P
THAT'S THE WAY LOVE GOES

"That's the Way Love Goes is fiction with many movements, an ambitious multi-angled view of the lives of young black men and the choices they make as they head into adulthood."
Kenji Jasper, author of *Dark* and *Dakota Grand*

"The relationship drama in this novel made my time in the Outback seem like a cakewalk. Engrossing and hilarious!"
Nick Brown, *Survivor: Australian Outback* Castaway

"Marvelous, mesmerizing, and utterly masculine! *That's the Way Loves Goes*—the title says it all. Daryl C. Diggs is the perfect guide to take you down the winding path that love travels. Follow Donavin and Jasmine as they navigate tantalizing twists and turns, potential potholes, and funny forks in the road on their way to a happy and loving relationship. With fresh characters and gripping prose, Daryl C. Diggs shows the way love goes after it leaves the heart."
Byron Harmon, author of *All the Women I've Loved* and three-time Emmy award-winning Executive Producer, WTTG Fox 5

"With vivid characters and comical situations, *That's the Way Love Goes* is a refreshingly unique romantic comedy."
Nancey Flowers, author of *A Fool's Paradise* and *Shattered Vessels*

"A storytelling masterpiece. A great start from a promising young author!"
MarkQuat Mathis, CEO and President, Soul 7 Entertainment, Inc.

"Billion Dollar Playboy Donavin Jackson and Jasmine DeRoche find out just how love goes in *That's the Way Love Goes*. With all the ensuing drama, not to mention laughs, you will not want to put this book down."
Mina Harris, Royalty Administration Analyst, Recording Industry Association of America

THAT'S THE WAY LOVE GOES

A NOVEL BY

DARYL C. DIGGS

Dianum
Entertainment

Published by Dianum Entertainment
244 Fifth Avenue, Suite B204
New York, New York 10001-7604

Printed in Canada
Second Printing
10 9 8 7 6 5 4 3 2

Designed by ATWR Designs

Publisher's Cataloging-in-Publication
(Provided by Quality Books, Inc.)

Diggs, Daryl C.

That's the way love goes / by Daryl C. Diggs.
p.cm.
LCCN 2002091683
ISBN 0-972-02800-5

1.African Americans—Fiction.   I.Title

PS3604.I5663T43 2002   813.6
                                                QBI33-454

darylcdiggs@aol.com
Visit: http://www.darylcdiggs.com

ACKNOWLEDGMENTS

It's like 3 a.m., y'all. If I forgot anybody, please blame my head and not my heart.

First and foremost, I'd like to thank Almighty God. With Him all things are possible. My family: James Diggs; Connie Diggs; and Keith Diggs. You've given me the foundation with which to become a man. I am eternally grateful to you all!

Mo' family: The memory of Leona Headley; Headleys; Owens; Cowans; Evans (not the one from *Good Times*); Montanezes; Watkins; Ellises; Beazers; Alstons; Harmons; Williams; McCarrons; the memory of Cornelius Begley, Sr.; Begleys; Morehouse College; Christian Brothers Academy; Taunton School; Sponsors For Educational Opportunity; INROADS; and Black Writers Alliance.

Kimberly Hines and Tia Shabazz—This would not have been a reality without the two of you. Thank you for the phenomenal job you've done in editing *That's The Way Love Goes*. Pentouch represent!

Josh Patterson—Thanks for the logo design.

Twig One Stop—Thanks for the cover design.

Special acknowledgement to all those who lost their lives on September 11th.

Shout outs (in no particular order): Jason Beazer (love ya like a play cousin); Marc Alston (stop singin' in the hallway already); Uncle Buddy (for breakin' down the business); Jelani Watkins; Curtis Brown; Brian Carter (I'm sure you realize your contribution); Brandon Johnson; Jerome Beazer; Jerrell Love; Antonio Alston; Nilaja Figueroa; Sam Figueroa; Justin P (keep ya head up); Dahniel "Starks" Buie; Chris Aiken; Rasean Evans; Nick "The Goat" Brown; Johnny Moore; Derrick Cameron; Greg Schmidt; Lee Braughton; Rich Harvey; Gooch; Liz Valerio; Maurice Hendrix; Rafique DeCastro; Ray Connell; Maya Headley; Chris Gibson; Ebony Daniels (stop killing r's); Leonard Stephens; Milly Calderon; Trae Byrd; Vanita Gaonkar;

Nefertiti Jones (Diva! Cop da album, y'all!); Wendy Weiser; Allen Boomer; Jeanine Barnett; Nailah Flake; Raughn Turner; Anne Prior; Kara Findlay; Brenda Ramos; Alexis Palmer; Terri Lewis; Jaimee Fomer; Teresa Spitzer; Rona Morrissette (for giving me so much damn material to work with); Xavier Bost; Jamellah Ellis; Sarah Curtis-Bey (all this drama over a snowboard?); Melle Hocke; Melissa March; Rachana Khandelwal; Tamiko Shell; Lauren Copeland; Rosa Lira; Nidhi Chandra; Sabrina Saraf; Terese and Heather Tarantino; Britt Hogue; Jasmine Montez (for gettin' me started again—kismet); Rupal Naik; Dyah Goodman; Mike Parks; the twins, Erissa and Carmen Reeves; Devin Colón; Rasean and Rashad Hodge; Keith "The Deacon" Camper; Kathy Walden; Tamara and Sabrina Gobin; Ivy Jack; Stephen Espinosa; Faisal Sharwani; Melanie Lawrence; Nicola Halsal; Jason Anthony; Kenny Pitts; all the cats from Cell Block 2; Tamisha Scott; Jane Mitchell; Jack Williams; Nicole Franklin; Kenisha West; Khanequa Tuitt; Leslie McClain; Lee Vert Holmes; Mondella Jones; Ron Kavanaugh; Tony Woods; Chris Tengi; David Shickler; Josh King; John Pokorny; Barbara Jackson; Tiombe Knucklos; Devin Johnson; Lenny Hypolite; Jessica Kusner; Melia Prushnok; Brother Michael and Brother Augustin (for keeping me halfway sane through high school); Darlene C.; Monica K.; Shinelle; Lindsey Coco; Meghan Hutchesson; Sean Nunan (for being brave enough to have us read *The Autobiography of Malcolm X* in high school. With four black kids at my high school, that was mad gangsta!); Danielle Randazzo; Shelley Schick; George Wells; Maurice Dobson; Chris Raymond; Martha Leighton; Olga Gomer; Eric Saxon; Jehu Eaves; Shaka Rasheed; Keith Spelmon; Malick Diop; Nigel Lewis; Kenji Jasper; Lo; Philip McNeal; Ben McLaurin; Belinda White; Keith Hollingsworth; Jacques Sexton; Charlene Jackson; Nancey Flowers; Angel Stewart; Antoinette Roach; Tiffany Lowery; Erika Smith; Judith Cruz; Dustin DePalma; Thomas Roberts; Evelyn Rodrigues;

Iveta Holikova; Mr. Harris; Mr. Marshall; Marcus Major; KP; Wiz; Haze; Sewnig; Mulligan; Maier; McKenna; Ravi; The Soleil Group; Dalia Zaza; Nicole Adams; Carron Allen; Arlene; Yee Kee Lam; Freddy Menjivar; Monika Martinez; Niki Hundlani; Verushka Cruz; Barbara Keaton; Eric Jerome Dickey; Parry Brown; and thanks to all the folks at my job. Big up to the Hub!

Never let your attitude doom your reality
Never forget what is most important to you
Never let the negative energy of others influence
how you feel about yourself
Never forget the people who got you to where you are
Always be true to you

—Daryl C. Diggs

CHAPTER
ONE

"Damn, I got it going on."

The streetlight changed unnoticed as Donavin stood admiring his reflection in the window of an upscale boutique. His light brown eyes took in the cream linen shirt and black slacks that, although off the rack from a downtown New York boutique, hung as if tailored to fit his muscular 6'3" frame. "I'm gonna get so much play tonight y'all are gonna be left on the bench."

Adam Witherspoon cleared his throat and stepped in front of his friend to get a better look at himself. "Surely you jest. You're hardly as handsome and dashing as myself, my brother." He confirmed that there wasn't one strand of his curly hair out of place and smoothed his tapered sideburns. "Furthermore, as you're well aware, Spoon scoops all the ladies."

"Y'all some conceited bastards," J.R. drawled in his unmistakable New Orleans twang. "Both y'all gon' come up short. Us darkskinned bruthas been in fuh da past nine, ten years." J.R. stepped in front of Spoon and Donavin, easily eclipsing them both with his thick football player's build. "Ladies love da chocolate, and da chocolate loves da ladies."

Donavin and Spoon looked at each other and shook their heads. They moved around to stand on either side of J.R. "Whatever, man," Donavin said. "We all look good like the Billion Dollar Playboys should."

"My sentiments exactly." Spoon dapped Donavin.

"Fuh sho. Deez breezies ain't even ready fuh da BDP," J.R. added.

The light changed, and they reluctantly left their reflections behind to cross the street. Although it was August, the cool black men barely broke a sweat as they strode down Wall Street to attend the end-of-summer networking reception sponsored by the firms at which they'd interned that summer. In a matter of weeks they'd be back in Atlanta starting their senior year at Stratford University, the nation's leading historically black university. In the meantime they had their minds on the honeys and the honeys on their minds.

Networking with established businesspeople was supposed to be the theme of the event. Instead the scene typically turned into one of people trying to make dates instead of business connections.

Holding court the way they were at the open bar was more than the three men could have hoped for. With the sea of fine, employed women parading around the room, they had their picks of tall, short, thick, or slim in shades of chocolate, caramel, butterscotch, and French vanilla. All thirty-one flavors seemed to be well represented.

"It's an exciting day in the Big Apple, sports fans," Spoon quipped in his best sports announcer imitation. He held one hand over his ear; his eyes scanned the room. "The Billion Dollar Playboys are about to put it on the working girls of New York City."

"How right you are, sir. I'm glad I brought my A-game as usual," Donavin added.

J.R. scowled. "Dawg, you steady be talkin' dat junk. Please show me sumthin'. Put up some numbers on da court 'stead of talkin' dat shit in da locker room."

"When I see one who is worthy of the Donavin Jackson experience, I'll be sure to let you know. Country muthafucka."

"Why I got to be country, dawg?"

"Because of that thick ass accent you sport, *dawg*," Donavin mocked.

"You a wild boy, D. You funnier than a one-legged man at an ass-kickin' contest."

"Fellas! You guys need to focus on the task at hand," Spoon interrupted. "All these lonely women needing to be held and caressed and kissed and sucked and—"

"Okay, okay, too much information, Spoon." Donavin threw up his hand to silence him. "You need to hold that down. Everybody doesn't need to know how freak-nasty you really are."

"Yeah, dawg! Have a drink and cool yo' hormones, man!"

"Whatever. You two stand here and converse with one another if you like. I'm going to work the room if you can smell what the Spoon is cookin'." Spoon strolled off with his Manhattan in hand.

"Why does Spoon think he's The Rock?" Donavin shook his head.

"He be watchin' dat wrasslin' every week, dawg. I can't front. Dat shit be off da hook sometimes. Dem wrasslers be like modern day gladiators, bruh. Speakin' a which, dat movie was so damn hard! Maximus was a straight killa."

"Well, one thing he said is correct. We need to start stepping to some of these young ladies instead of talking to each other."

"Dat's real, playa. I'll holla at yo' ass later." J.R. picked up his Jack and Coke off the bar and made his way to a chatting group of ladies.

Donavin began to case the room to see who would be the object of his attention for the evening. He sauntered about like he owned the place and enjoyed a private chuckle when he overheard three women admiring him as he passed.

"Damn!"

"He is *foine*!"

"Girl, you ain't neva lied."

Donavin continued his self-confident stride until *she* walked in. His smile was knocked off balance. He stopped and did a double take. He had only taken a few sips of his Thug Passion, a concoction made of Hennessey and Alizé, so he knew he wasn't drunk. His eyes drank in the leggy caramel beauty. She wore a fitted business suit that stopped mid-thigh and accentuated all of her curves. Her face, framed by long jet-black hair, was angelic. There was something familiar about her, but he couldn't place it. Where had he seen her before? In a movie? On TV? In his dreams?

Donavin contemplated his approach. The sista was banging, but he had to see what her teeth looked like before he spit any game. He was very particular about his women. He valued intelligence along with drive and determination. Beauty and a great physique were definite pluses, but above all else she had to have good teeth.

In his experience he found that fine women with plenty of T and A came a dime a dozen. But a woman with all of those positive traits and nice teeth to boot would make him consider marriage. He'd had too many bad experiences where he'd meet a good-looking woman only to have his hopes dashed when she opened her mouth to display tobacco road.

Donavin stayed about ten paces behind to appear inconspicuous as he followed her around the room. After a few minutes of his trailing her, she still hadn't turned around. He maneuvered around her, orbiting like a satellite, to get a full frontal view. Several minutes elapsed with Donavin's patience.

"Will you smile so I can see your damn teeth, woman!" Donavin tapped his foot on the carpet.

Finally it happened. She ran into someone she knew, and the gates of heaven suddenly opened before his eyes.

"Yes! Thirty-two straight pearly whites." Donavin grinned. "Okay, Donavin, let's show that A-game you were talking about earlier." He strolled over to introduce himself as the other woman walked away.

Before he could drop one of his stellar first lines, she turned and said, "Donavin Jackson, I presume?"

He masked his surprise. "Very good. I don't believe I've had the pleasure."

"I guess a proper introduction would be appropriate. My name is Jasmine. Jasmine DeRoche." She extended her hand and Donavin enveloped it in both of his.

"It is a pleasure to make your acquaintance, Miss Jasmine DeRoche. I noticed you when you arrived. You're a very beautiful woman."

Jasmine smiled once again, opening the gates of heaven solely for Donavin this time. "Thank you. I've always heard that you're quite the charmer."

Now it was Donavin's turn to display his impeccable Billion Dollar Playboy smile. "I feel I'm at a disadvantage. You know my story, but I don't know yours. Where do we know each other from?"

"You're a senior at Stratford. I just graduated from there in May. You and your little crew are famous, or should I say infamous. I think I saw the other two in here when I came in. The Billion Dollar Playboys, right?"

Embarrassed that Jasmine had just told him the part of his business he would have preferred she not know, Donavin offered a sheepish grin. "That's just a little inside joke. We're just a small group of gentlemen who live life to the fullest. I believe, however, we do it with a tad more style than most."

"Style, huh?"

"Clearly I think one should live with a little *je ne sais quoi*, a little *joie de vie*, if you will."

Jasmine laughed. "You are too funny. So, what are you doing in New York this summer?"

"A little internship in private banking at Proctor and Proctor," Donavin said nonchalantly.

"Nice."

"Yourself?"

"I'm a consultant at Simon and Rothstein."

"Impressive. So, Miss Jasmine, what do you do for fun?"

"Is that a proposal, Mr. Donavin?"

Donavin was slightly taken aback. He didn't think that it would be this easy with a woman this fine. "Why, yes, Jasmine. I'd love the opportunity to entertain you for an evening."

"Just an evening?" Jasmine raised an eyebrow and smirked. "Is that honestly all you can handle?"

Donavin leaned close to whisper in Jasmine's ear. "How about you slip me your number, and we'll see *just how much I can handle.*"

"Touché." Jasmine reached into her Kate Spade purse to retrieve her business card case. She jotted her home and cell numbers on the back of the card and handed it to him. "I don't like to waste cards, so I expect you to call and not just brag to your boys about how many numbers you got tonight. Are we clear?"

"So cynical. We'll have to work on that."

Jasmine looked Donavin up and down then met his eyes once again. "We have a few things to work on." She smiled and walked off without so much as a goodbye, but her body language said all that needed to be stated.

"Damn," Donavin mumbled, "did that just happen?"

J.R. and Spoon walked over just in time to watch Jasmine walk away.

Spoon smiled widely. "Action Jackson has done it again."

"Fuh sho. Dat's a hot ass girl," J.R. chimed in. "What did she do? Ask you if you knew me?"

"That, gentlemen, was Jasmine DeRoche. Says she graduated from Stratford this year. I don't know how I missed a woman that fine. Do either of you remember her?"

"You know, as a matter of fact I do," Spoon answered. "She used to sing in the glee club. Remember I was the treasurer freshman year. You guys remember, right?"

Donavin and J.R. shot a "who gives a damn" look at one another.

"Anyway, she was rather plain jane-ish back then, but she must have started drinking milk or something."

"Dawg, did you git da digits? Wait, lemme rephrase dat. Dawg, tell me you got da digits," J.R. probed.

"Would I be a Billion Dollar Playboy if I didn't?"

CHAPTER TWO

Donavin was used to being in control when he approached a woman. Although Jasmine had definitely turned the game around on him, he knew he would have pursued her even if she hadn't willingly given him her number.

He tapped his fingers on the desk. A spreadsheet stared at him from his computer screen, but his focus was on the business card lying on his blotter.

It had been two days and Jasmine occupied every corner of his thoughts. He hadn't called her at home that Friday night like he wanted to. Although eager to connect with her again, he wasn't going to play himself. He had a reputation to uphold. Obviously a skilled player as well, Jasmine had won round one, but Donavin was determined to come back strong for round two. He picked up the phone and dialed her number.

"Simon and Rothstein, Jasmine DeRoche speaking."

"Good morning, Simon and Rothstein Jasmine DeRoche speaking."

Jasmine knitted her eyebrows; it was too early in the morning for telephone games. "Who's calling, please?" she asked stiffly.

Donavin chuckled. "This is Donavin Jackson. How are you this beautiful morning?"

"Oh hey, Donavin." Jasmine softened. "Woo, I'm so tired. Mondays are a beast. Thank the good Lord for coffee."

"You're a coffee drinker?"

"I'm trying to cut down, but on Mondays I'm just like fuck it."

She said that curse word and scored major cool points with Donavin. He hated women who were so prissy, prim, and proper that they thought cursing was beneath them.

"I'm not a fan of Mondays either, but I usually shake off my fatigue by the evening. Would you care to join me tonight to check out an open mic at a coffee spot in the Village?"

"Very smooth how you took my appreciation of coffee and turned it into a date opportunity. You are as impressive as your reputation suggests."

"We're going to have to talk about this reputation thing. I think that someone has been giving you some false information on the kid."

"Anyway, what time should I be ready?" Jasmine ignored his last comment.

"So you accept?"

"Yes, keep up with the conversation, sweetie."

Donavin smiled into the receiver. He always appreciated a good game of verbal fencing and liked the challenge Jasmine offered.

"How about producing yourself at eight o'clock? Can you handle that or will you be preparing more of your little one-liners?"

This time Jasmine was taken aback. Most of the guys who approached her were only into kissing her behind and telling her how wonderful she was. It was refreshing for her to encounter a man with a backbone.

Jasmine laughed. "No, I prep my one-liners on Sunday night for the entire week. I usually get off at about six. I work in the financial district downtown, so I'm close to my apartment in Brooklyn. I can be ready by eight. Are you picking me up or are we meeting in the Village?"

"A true gentlemen always picks up a lady."

"I live in Brooklyn at . . . hold on one second." She placed him on hold briefly and finished telling him the address a moment later. "Do you know where that is?"

"No, but you'll find that I'm extremely resourceful."

"Hmm, if you say so. Listen, I've gotta run, but I'll see you later."

"Yes, you will. Eight sharp."

"Bye, Donavin."

Jasmine hung up on her end, and Donavin rested the receiver in its cradle on his. For the first time in a long time, Donavin was excited about a prospect. Jasmine's ability to tantalize him physically and mentally was rare. He didn't want to get too caught up, but he had a good feeling about her—one he hadn't felt in a while. He picked the phone back up to share his progress with Spoon.

"Good morning. Dillon Capital Partners, Adam Witherspoon speaking. How may I be of service?" Spoon answered in his best corporate Negro voice.

"Hey, man, it's D. I just set up a date with old girl from the reception last Friday."

"Kudos, my friend, kudos. What you plan on getting into?"

"A little open mic at the Nubian Winds Poets Café in the Village. Not quite sure what to do afterward, though."

"Myself, being a man of our town, would be most honored to give you some suggestions. After the open mic, I'd stop by Justin's. It's a cool spot to have a drink and you might see Puffy or P. Diddy, whichever you choose to call him. Then you simply must take a horse-and-carriage ride in Central Park. After the carriage ride, she'll be more than ready, believe me."

"What's with this 'man of our town' stuff? You're from Long Island. Not exactly the same thing. I appreciate the help, though.

You're truly a wealth of information."

"Glad to be of service, my good man. I expect a full report in the morning. Represent the BDP to the fullest."

"Always."

Donavin rushed to finish his work so he could mentally prepare for the date. He would have to get some gear and find out where the hell she lived. He was, however, a member of the BDP—they never stress; they adapt.

The day seemed to drag on and on, but six o'clock finally came and Donavin hurried uptown to Spoon and J.R.'s place. They lived in student housing at Columbia University's East Campus dorm on West 116th Street, as did most of the summer interns. He kept a few extra clothes there so that he wouldn't always have to go home to Short Hills to change. Donavin chose to stay at home with his parents in the affluent New Jersey suburb during the summer because he liked having someone else do his laundry and he loved his mother's cooking.

After taking a taxicab to Columbia, Donavin paid the driver and made his way into the building. The security guard in the lobby allowed him to enter, and Donavin walked up to his friends' suite. He impatiently knocked on their door and J.R. answered seconds later.

"What up, dawg? What brings you to da neighborhood?"

"What's up, playboy? I need to grab some of my gear for the evening."

J.R. stepped aside to let Donavin in. "Where you goin' tonight? I ain't say you could go out."

"I'm going out with that girl from the other night."

"Da one wit' da big ol' donkey ass? You win so big! You a straight-up pimp!"

"Tell me something I don't know, Big Country."

"Hey, bruh, you ain't got too many mo' country jokes left befo' you get some smackdown laid ·on ya."

"You've been watching wrestling with Spoon again, haven't you?"

"Hell yeah, man. Dem story lines be so good. Best thang on TV. Guaranteed. You need to git down wit' it."

Donavin shook his head. "Hmm. Let's see. Beautiful girl? Wrestling? Beautiful girl? Wrestling? Now if it was beautiful girls wrestling it might be different. You lose; I gotta get dressed."

"Good. I got company comin' anyway. Don't need you over here blockin'."

Donavin showered and dressed. He put on a pair of black Perry Ellis pants, a gray short-sleeved Armani shirt, and black Kenneth Cole shoes—his trademark style from head to toe. A splash of Ralph Lauren Romance and he was ready to go.

Donavin said his goodbyes to J.R. "All right, sir, I'm out. Enjoy the wrestling match, and I don't mean the one on TV."

They gave each other dap. "Aight, playa, do yo' thang and make da BDP proud. I know I will."

CHAPTER THREE

Donavin walked up to the door of Jasmine's brownstone and buzzed her apartment. Without asking who it was, Jasmine replied over the intercom, "I'll be right down, Donavin."

Minutes later she appeared in a sexy black dress with spaghetti straps and an asymmetrical hem. The dress wrapped itself around her figure. As she got closer, Donavin caught the scent of one of his favorite perfumes. She was wearing Amarige, which threw his olfactory into overdrive. All of this, combined with the heels, hair, and makeup, made her the picture of perfection.

"Good evening, Miss Jasmine. You look rather exquisite." He hoped he did not sound as blown away as he felt.

Blushing, Jasmine replied, "Thank you. You have an eye for fashion yourself. You look very . . . cute."

"Cute? I'm a member of the BDP, sweetie. We're smooth, stylish, refined, debonair." Donavin struck a few exaggerated modeling poses. "Cute is not in the repertoire."

"Oh my God, you are so conceited!"

"Au contraire, mademoiselle. Not conceited, confident. Say it with me—*con-fi-dent*."

Jasmine rolled her eyes and placed her hands on her waist.

"Issues. Say it with me—*is-sues*. Come on. Let's go."

She took his hand and Donavin felt a jolt from her touch. They stepped to the curb and hailed a cab. During the entire ride to Manhattan, Donavin found it difficult to keep his eyes off of her crossed legs. It was hard for him not to imagine how her shapely calves would feel wrapped around him, but he tried his best to make small talk.

"So, Jasmine, you've said a few things about my crew. How is it that you escaped my attention in school?"

"Well, I didn't party that much, and I didn't wear the Black College Female Uniform."

"What uniform might that be?"

"You know, dressed in black from head to toe. Tight black baby tee, tight black pants, and black boots. It was ridiculous. I always felt like I should be directing girls to the Fly Girl auditions or something."

Donavin laughed because that was what he had been chasing for the previous three years.

"I remember when you were dating one of my classmates, Crystal Armstrong. She fit the stereotype to a T."

"Crystal Armstrong. I haven't heard that name in a second. Come on now. You have to give me a bio or something. All of this one-sided information has got to go."

The cab driver alerted them that they had reached their destination and Jasmine asked, "Why on earth would I ever give up my advantage over you?" and deftly exited the cab.

They walked toward the Nubian Winds Café in silence. A million thoughts ran through Donavin's mind. He was more than attracted to her, but the fact that she seemed to be in control really bothered him. She knew more details about his past than he cared for her to know.

Jasmine had different thoughts on her mind. She knew

Donavin's story so well because she had been interested in him in college but was too shy to approach. Even though he was younger, she admired his style, class, and ease. That unmistakable presence of his made a big impression on her. Jasmine figured that if she brought the game to him instead of vice versa, she would seem more interesting to him. From the looks of things, she was correct.

The couple entered the café just as the open mic session was getting underway. The room was dimly lit, and the flicker of candles made the room seem to glow. They sat down at a table that allowed them to see the whole room. Donavin always insisted on this because he wanted to be in a position that allowed him to see who was coming and going and what was going on. Then again, the only one he needed to keep his eye on was seated right across from him.

"This is very nice, Donavin. Take all of your dates here?"

"I wouldn't waste a place like this on any woman that didn't stand up to your standard of beauty and refinement," Donavin countered.

Jasmine tried not to blush, but it was over. Donavin had a knack for making a woman feel like no one else existed. His eyes told her that he was sincere.

The stage was being set up for the next performer and Norman Brown's instrumental version of Janet Jackson's "That's the Way Loves Goes" began to play as a gap filler.

Jasmine closed her eyes and said, "Mmm. That's my song." She then stood up at the table and began to dance and sing to Donavin over the track.

"You've got some pipes, girl." Donavin smiled. He was pleasantly surprised by her impromptu performance.

Jasmine continued, and her fan base seemed to grow larger. All attention shifted to her. After a couple more minutes she finished her rendition of Janet's smooth classic and took a bow.

"Encore!" a patron at the next table shouted. Jasmine received a standing ovation from the entire café.

"Go 'head, Miss Jackson." Donavin stood and applauded her.

Jasmine gave a shy smile as if she were embarrassed by the attention she was getting. She settled back into her chair.

"I hope you were comparing me to Janet when you called me Miss Jackson. This is only our first date, and I don't see my ring."

Donavin laughed. "No, I called you Miss Jackson because I'm a nasty boy."

"I heard that about you."

"Spoon told me that you were in the glee club when you were in school, but I didn't expect you to blow like that."

Jasmine ran her fingers through her hair. "I try to do a little somethin' somethin' every once in a while."

Donavin gazed directly in to her eyes. "What other hidden talents do you possess?"

As they sat and conversed more, the banter seemed to flow naturally. They laughed and felt as comfortable as if they had known each other for years. After a while they became lost in the stir of echoes that consumed the room. The beauty of the beating drum accompanied with the poetry of the spoken word performances created an air of sensuality that engulfed them both.

Around midnight, the set ended and they took the opportunity to go on that horse-and-carriage ride in the park. But first, Donavin wanted to stop by a liquor store to get a bottle of Cabernet Sauvignon. They did so, and just before Donavin reached out his hand to hail a cab, Jasmine said, "You might think this is really ghetto, but let's hit up Popeye's for a snack. I have a craving for some wings."

Donavin was pleasantly surprised at Jasmine's suggestion. If a guy ever decided to take a first date to Popeye's, chances were that he would not get a second one.

They took a cab to Popeye's on Seventh Avenue and they were the best-dressed couple in the joint. They munched on greasy chicken and buttery biscuits, then hopped another cab to Central Park for the carriage ride. They forgot to get cups at the restaurant so they had to drink wino style—directly from the bottle. Each of them took large swigs and finished the bottle in less than five minutes. It took another five minutes for the alcohol to take effect, then they loosened up and their frisky hands began to acquaint themselves with each other's bodies. Donavin tickled Jasmine and she pinched him in return. Her hands traveled straight down his chest to his crotch.

"Hey now!" Donavin pulled back. "It's like that?"

She answered with a drunken giggle. Donavin proceeded to softly squeeze Jasmine's nipple through her dress.

"Hey, you can't do that. You have to at least kiss me before you go titty-squeezing," Jasmine slurred.

Donavin required no further invitation, and the two locked lips and embraced for what seemed like hours. Though inebriated, the kiss was very intense and both of them knew it was going to happen at some point in the evening. The passionate exchange ended only when the driver of the carriage informed them that the ride was over and suggested that perhaps they should get a room.

They stumbled from the carriage onto the curb. Jasmine teetered on her heels and Donavin held her up.

"Mmm, D, where did you learn to kiss like that?"

"I just do what I do."

"Yes, you certainly do." Jasmine yawned and stretched. Her round breasts pressed against the fabric of her dress. "What time is it? We have to go to work tomorrow. We have to go home."

Donavin looked at his Rolex watch. "It's like . . . oh shit, it's a quarter to two. Fuck! I missed my bus back to Jersey."

Jasmine instantly felt guilty. "Oh, no! I'm sorry. It's my fault. You can stay with me tonight. But you have to stay on the couch. No funny business, okay?"

Donavin was a little tipsy, but not as drunk as Jasmine. He knew that he could've stayed at his boys' dorm or even caught the last bus back to Jersey if he really tried to. However, she'd extended the invitation and he was curious to see where the evening would lead.

During the cab ride back to Jasmine's apartment, Jasmine rested her head on Donavin's chest—partly because her head was still spinning and partly because she enjoyed being close to him.

They got back to her place shortly after two. Donavin paid the driver, then carried Jasmine up the two flights of stairs to her apartment. Jasmine had to muster all of her strength just to open the door. Donavin surveyed the apartment as Jasmine flicked on the lights. The apartment was a well-decorated one-bedroom unit with leather furniture and a nice entertainment system. Jasmine obviously had a thing for Ernie Barnes. She had the popular painting from the '70's sitcom *Good Times* hanging on her wall along with many of his other works. She also had a great deal of family pictures scattered about.

Jasmine led Donavin to her bedroom where there was a large queen-size bed with an oak frame opposite a small sofa. She handed him a blanket and pillow and ushered him to the sofa.

Donavin had his game face on. *Damn! I didn't think she was serious about having a brother sleep on the couch. Whatever. I'm here and that's half the battle.*

He slowly stripped down to his Polo boxers, exposing his finely tuned physique, and took his place on the couch without even a hint of an attitude.

Jasmine fidgeted with her alarm clock and tried to pretend she wasn't watching him out of the corner of her eye. She then dimmed the lamp on her nightstand and disappeared into her bathroom, reappearing minutes later wearing a black Dolce & Gabbana tank top and a pair of matching lace panties.

Donavin had fallen into a light slumber, but he stirred slightly when she came back into the room. His eyes focused on her form and he snapped awake, holding his body as still as possible.

Oh, no the hell she didn't! She's going to wear something like that and have my black ass over here? Play it cool, man, play it cool.

"Goodnight, Jas. I had a wonderful time with you this evening."

Wonderful time? Half my body is falling out of this outfit and that's all he has to say? Do I need to write it down for him?

"Goodnight, D. I had a wonderful time, too."

She lit a single candle beside her bed, then turned out the lamp. The flame cast a seductive glow on her silhouette.

Donavin rolled over, turning his back to her. *Oh well. No play tonight.*

A few minutes passed and Jasmine began to toss and turn as if trying to find a comfortable spot. He knew this was a sign, but if she wanted company she was going to have to ask for it.

Jasmine moaned softly. "Donavin, are you asleep?"

"Huh? What?" Donavin pretended she woke him. He was now practically sober and knew what was up.

Jasmine propped herself up on her elbows. "You look uncomfortable. Why don't you take the other side of the bed?"

"Aight, Jas. If you insist."

He got up and crawled into the bed, still playing it cool. He made sure he left a good amount of space between himself and Jasmine.

"You're so far away, Donavin. Aren't you cold? Come closer."

Donavin played along and inched closer to Jasmine, firmly pressing his body against hers. He wrapped his arm around her. She scooted closer, pushing her behind into his crotch, then she slowly began to grind. Jasmine took his right hand and placed it on her stomach, then slowly guided it to her breasts. The whole while she remained firmly ensconced against his now erect penis. She placed his hand between her moistening thighs.

I love it when the plan comes together. A smile radiated across his face. "Oh, Donavin."

"Lay on your stomach."

She did as told and Donavin sat up. He began to massage and kiss her neck and shoulders, then slowly inched his fingers down her back. Jasmine squirmed under his touch, releasing more sounds of pleasure. Donavin marveled at how smooth and soft her skin was. The aroma of her perfume consumed him, and he could think of nothing but having her.

"Turn over, Jasmine."

She rolled over and now lay on her back. Donavin moved on top of her and they kissed passionately. He reached for the waistband of her panties. She grabbed his hand.

"Donavin, stop. Oh my God, I really want to, but you can't have it on the first date. You just can't."

"Look, I know this is our first date, but having sex is just a means of getting intimate with that special someone. We're both mature, consenting adults. Everything is cool."

Damn. I even amaze myself with the lines I come up with sometimes. After that speech, I would give it to me for sure. His ego swelled.

Donavin rained passionate kisses down her neck as he felt her body begin to relax beneath him. Again he reached for her waistband to remove her panties.

Jasmine stiffened slightly, caressed his cheeks, and gently kissed his lips and then his forehead. She crossed her arms against his chest. "Sorry, big boy. You are *not* scoring tonight!"

She couldn't help but laugh and Donavin followed. They kissed for a few moments more and fell asleep in each other's arms.

After three short hours of sleep they awoke to the alarm clock's annoying buzz. Jasmine hit the snooze button with a purpose and yawned. "Looks like we gotta get up." She shook Donavin gently.

He sat up and stretched. "Yeah, I have to run to Spoon and J.R.'s to get a suit for work."

Donavin pecked Jasmine softly on the lips and stood. He dipped into the bathroom for a few minutes then came back out to get dressed.

Jasmine watched him pull his clothes on. *Damn, maybe I should have given him some.*

She got up to get a robe from her closet and then led him to the front door.

"Are you disappointed?"

"Not at all. You were perfect. A night I won't soon forget."

"Should I expect to hear from you?"

"Maybe. If you're lucky." Donavin winked at her and gave a cocky smile.

"Really?" Jasmine countered. "I know somebody who didn't exactly get lucky last night."

"Oh, you got jokes, huh? Who's to say it was my loss and not yours, Baby Girl?"

"If it does ever happen . . ." Jasmine threw her arms around his neck and seductively whispered in his ear. "I promise you that you'll fully understand you were the lucky one."

CHAPTER
FOUR

Later that morning, Donavin sat at his desk looking up stock quotes, but once again Jasmine permeated his thoughts. He was a pretty tough critic of females and he was already enamored with her—the way she moved, the way she talked, and the way she carried herself all impressed him very much. He found himself wanting more—much more. Although he wanted to sex her, he respected the fact that she'd resisted his advances.

The telephone rang, snapping Donavin out of deep thought. He picked up after the second ring. "Good morn—"

"What up, dawg?" J.R. cut him off. "Look, I ain't got time fuh no long-winded conversation, so tell me what happened wit' dat big-booty girl. You said you couldn't talk when I saw yo' black ass dis mornin'. What happened?"

"Must you be so uncouth?"

"What part of I ain't got time fuh no long-winded conversation did you not understand, playa? I know you must have messed wit' her 'cause you didn't go home last night. Yo' momma called me looking fuh yo' ass. Da drawers were what color, you said?"

"Oh yeah, I've been meaning to call her. Can I tell you what happened later when I have some freedom to talk?"

"You hit it, didn't you? Dat's my boy! Hoodie hoo!"

Donavin yawned and shook his head. "I promise to fill you in later on what I can."

"What you can?" J.R.'s question was loaded with attitude. "Tonight we goin' fuh drinks and yo' ass is gon' give us da sex-down details."

"Fine. Call Spoon and tell him to meet us at Windows on the World at seven."

"See ya den, playboy."

Donavin struggled to stay awake for the rest of the day. As quitting time approached, however, he got an added boost of energy at the prospect of seeing his friends. He gathered his Coach briefcase and left the office.

At Windows on the World on the top floor of Tower One of the World Trade Center, Donavin joined Spoon and J.R. at their table. "Good evening, gentlemen."

J.R. took a big gulp of Hennessey and Coke. "Fuck pleasantries. All I wanna hear is a story pertainin' to dat big-booty girl."

"Yes, Donavin, that would seem to be the appropriate topic of conversation. Please sit down and tell us what happened."

"A true gentlemen never reveals his escapades with a young lady," Donavin said, a sly smile blanketing his face.

J.R signaled for the waitress to come over to their table. "Dawg, if you don't order a drink and tell me what happened you 'bout to be da recipient of much smackdown."

"I'll have a glass of red wine," Donavin told the waitress. As she left with his order, J.R. and Spoon stared at Donavin, both tapping their fingers on the table in anticipation.

"Man," Donavin finally said, "I've got to tell you guys. Jasmine is off the hook for real."

"Got dang, I knew it! You hit dat big ol' donkey ass! Knowing good and well you northern boys can't handle no ass like dat. Ass like dat take a big southern playa like myself to ride it like a big ol' stallion." J.R. stood up and pretended to be riding a horse—complete with sound effects.

Spoon and Donavin burst out laughing. The waitress came back with Donavin's wine and fought to keep a straight face at the sight of J.R.

"Man, will you sit your sophomoric ass down. No, I didn't hit it."

"Then what did you mean when you said she's 'off the hook'?" Spoon wondered aloud.

"I don't know how to explain it. She has some kind of intangible quality. I couldn't just hit that and leave it."

"How would you know?"

"Fuck you, Spoon, but good looking out on the carriage ride."

"No problem. Did you guys make it to Justin's?"

"No, we skipped that and went to Popeye's, of all places."

J.R. chimed in. "Y'all are boring me so big right now. You quite clearly spent da night at ol' girl's crib. I don't know what you talkin' 'bout some greasy ass chicken fuh."

"Did you get some last night, Mr. Big Country? Mr. All-I-Do-Is-Talk-Shit?" Donavin snapped back.

"I beat it up so big last night. I had dat broad screamin' my name. 'Ooh J.R.' dis, 'ooh J.R.' dat. She couldn't git enough. If I asked dat girl to marry me today she'd say yes. Guaranteed!"

Donavin and Spoon laughed once again. "You are, without a doubt, the greatest, J.R.," Spoon said once he caught his breath. "I saw her briefly when I came in last night. Very nice, if I may say so myself. What was her name again?"

J.R. answered indignantly, "It don't matter what her name was!"

"In other words he doesn't remember," Donavin kidded.

"Dat was dat broad Alicia Williams from my job. Her being a dime was clearly a bonus 'cause I'll hit a girl who's a five as long as she got a big ass. Either way I win!"

Spoon nodded and sipped his glass of merlot. "But back to you, Donavin. Tell us what went down."

"It wasn't about getting the sex, y'all. Even though I would have taken it if she had given it to me. We just connected."

"Like doggy style?" J.R. asked facetiously.

"Shut the hell up, Big Country. I'm trying to tell you guys the story. Stop making me laugh. I mean, she just had it going on. Her game was definitely on point. She had enough game to rival a member of the BDP."

J.R. and Spoon clamored in unison, "Ooh . . . love jones! Ooh!"

"Whipped on da pussy without even gittin' a taste," J.R. added.

"Shut up and let me finish. We got drunk as hell on the carriage ride and that was the first time we kissed. I went home with her and we just laid together."

"Naked?"

Donavin stared at his friend and said, "J.R., you are quite possibly the horniest dude in the world."

"Why thank you. It's hard when God done gave me all dis *tes-tos-tyrone* to satisfy all deez breezies wit', but I do it. In da end He'll bless me fuh it."

"You're going straight to hell. You know that, right?" Donavin said.

"Donavin, there are a few holes in your story. Nine times out of ten, a girl doesn't take you home on the first date and not give you a little something for your troubles. But it seems as if you really like this one, so I'll respect that for now."

"Shit, Spoon, we need to git dis fool back to Atlanta befo' he starts fallin' in love and wantin' to break up da BDP!"

Spoon nodded in agreement and nonchalantly looked at the vibrating two-way pager attached to his belt. "Well, fellas, I'm sufficiently drunk now. I'm going home to turn in."

"Drunk? Offa one drink? Lyin' ass Spoon! I saw you look down at yo' pager. I know dat's a broad. You ain't slick. You see slick and do da opposite."

"What can I say? Guilty as charged." Spoon left his part of the bill and dapped them up before exiting.

"You really like dis girl, D?"

"Yeah, man, she's just mad cool and sexy as hell."

"Dat's aight, I suppose. Normally you jus' dog deez broads out 'cause you decide you don't like dey feet or you find somethin' wrong wit' dey teeth. Aw shit, who's blowin' up my spot?" J.R. unclipped his two-way from his belt and displayed the number.

"Which one of your *breezies* is requesting you now?"

"Dat's Jennifer. Breezie workin' over dere at Jordan and Sons."

"Mmm hmm, and what will y'all be doing tonight?"

"Neva you mind. Stay outta grown folk business." J.R. began to laugh and do a little dance as he stood. "I'm gon' beat it up so big. I'm gon' smack it up, flip it, and rub it down!"

"Oh no!" Donavin finished his sentence. "Please get your ass away from me."

They paid the remainder of the tab, exchanged dap, and went their separate ways.

Jasmine sat at the bar of the Butta Cup Lounge in the Fort Greene section of Brooklyn with her girlfriends, Stacia and Carmen. They normally gathered there on Tuesdays after they volunteered at the after-school reading program at PS 20. Jasmine yawned and propped her head up with her arm on the bar.

"Why are you so tired, mami?" Carmen asked, her high-pitched Rosie Perez-like voice grating on Jasmine's eardrums.

"For someone so little, you are so loud, Carmen."

Carmen sucked her teeth at Jasmine's reference to her height. "I am 5'3", thank you very much. I got your little right here," she said, standing to point to her rotund Puerto Rican backside.

"If y'all must know, I had a date last night. Stacia, you remember Donavin Jackson from school?"

"You really went out with that young boy last night?" Stacia shook her head in disbelief.

"He's only a year younger, Stace."

"Who's Donavin Jackson?" Carmen had not attended Stratford.

Stacia flung her long blonde-streaked hair over her shoulder and leaned forward to give Carmen the scoop. "He's a college boy Jasmine's trying to get with."

"Please, Stacia! If he tried to talk to you, you'd have fucked him, and you may or may not have told either of us about it."

Carmen chuckled. "Oh, no she didn't go there on you, Stacia."

"Well, he does look good, and he does come from money so I may have given him a taste. But I don't think that young whippersnapper could handle what I would put on him. I'd have him wanting to call me his momma and shit."

"Shut up, Stacia. I can't believe how you act sometimes. Around guys you act all innocent, but we know you're giving it away like it's going out of style."

"Give it up, Stace. I think you struck a nerve, mami. So, what did you do with him last night, J?"

"We went to the Nubian Winds Poets Café in the Village and listened to some spoken word. Then we capped the evening with a carriage ride in Central Park. He's just really cool. A total gentleman. He opened the door for me, pulled out my chair, and hung on my every word."

Stacia rolled her eyes. "Girl, cut to the chase. He spent the night and put it on you, didn't he? What's his body like? I remember that he was in really good shape."

"Skip that, mami. How big was his thing? I can't stand it when a fine, sexy, strong man has a little *pinga*. It's like watching a really good movie and then the ending sucks."

"He's got a nice body, definitely in shape. Oh! He's got the prettiest light brown eyes I've ever seen. As far as his thing is concerned, I wouldn't want to spoil the evening by telling either of you two ho's all the details."

"Aw, how you gonna play us like that?" Stacia protested.

"If anybody could use some dick in her life it's you, mami."

"So, Donavin's got you open like that, huh? Are you going to see him again? I know he must be getting ready to head back to school."

"I'd like to see him again, but I know he's going back to school and all the girls are gonna sweat him because he'll be the big man on campus. I'll see how it goes."

"Mira girlfriend, if the boy got looks, got body, and got money, you might as well enjoy him while you can. I say fuck his fine ass. Fuck him until you can't get out of bed in the morning."

Stacia high-fived Carmen. "Okay! Get yours, girl! You might as well make yourself happy. Lord knows Allen ain't doing the job."

"And he never will. But anyway, I really like Donavin. I don't want to be a cheap screw. I just felt like our connection was worth more than that."

Stacia tried to reason with Jasmine. "I don't think you're being honest with yourself. Take his boys, for example. As big and fine as J.R. may be, he will stick his thing in anything. And Adam? Sexy as can be and a little smoother in his approach, I hear he's a big time player, too. These are his closest friends. How can you expect him to be any different? Dogs of a feather . . ."

"I don't know. I just hope and pray that he is different from his boys. Last night was just so magical. Something special happened the first time he held me close to him."

"Yeah, your panties got wet!" Carmen howled at her own joke.

Jasmine smiled. "You guys are horrible."

All three women conversed further about the events of the previous night and then decided to call it an evening. Jasmine couldn't handle another late night. As they were leaving, Stacia cautioned her.

"I hope you know what you're doing, Jas. I'm sure he does—he's had lots of practice."

Jasmine cut her eyes at Stacia's remark. "I just have to see what happens and see where his head is at."

Carmen nodded. "Just be careful, chica. You know what, I want to meet these guys. Hook it up, Jas."

"I'll ask him."

With that, they each departed. As Jasmine walked down the street, their words echoed in her mind. Donavin's reputation was truly that of a player and a ladies' man. Maybe she would be just another name on a long list of women. Maybe he simply wanted one last conquest before he went back to Atlanta. The very idea made her rather uncomfortable, but she found solace in the fact that she felt their evening together was somehow different. Either way, she was willing to see where the relationship would lead.

CHAPTER FIVE

"Hey, Momma, what's up?" Donavin kissed his mother on her cheek. She lounged comfortably on her La-Z-Boy easy chair in the living room flipping through a magazine.

"Hey, baby," she returned. "With all of those communication devices we pay for, have you forgotten how to use them?"

"I've just been hangin' out a little bit, Momma. You know you're still my number one girl." Donavin wrapped his arms around her shoulders.

"I love you, too, but don't use your little lines on me. I'm not some naïve twenty-one-year-old girl."

Mr. Jackson folded his newspaper in half. "Your mother's right. If we're paying for a two-way pager, cell phone, and your education, the least you can do is call and say where you are and what you're doing."

"My bad. I'll try to keep everyone in the loop better from now on."

"Thank you, baby." Mrs. Jackson rose from her chair and gently stroked her son's face. He kissed her hand.

"Donny, do you want to take your mother to a movie tonight?"

"You know I would, Momma, but I've hardly gotten any sleep

over the last few days, and I gotta get up early for work tomorrow. Maybe this weekend?"

"Okay, baby." Mrs. Jackson was a little disappointed. "We've already eaten. Your dinner is in the oven."

"Thanks, Momma, I can taste it already. I'm dreading how much I'm gonna miss your cooking when I go back to school next week." He kissed her cheek again and proceeded to the kitchen to get his dinner. He took an oven mitt from the drawer beside the stove and carried his food upstairs to his room. After finishing his delicious meal, he called Jasmine.

"Hey, gorgeous."

Recognizing the voice, Jasmine giggled. "Tyson, is that you again?"

"This ain't no damn Tyson!"

"I know, *Donavin*. I was just playing with you. What's up, sweetie?"

"I'm doing all right. I had a great time with a beautiful woman last night."

"What did I tell you about seeing other women?" she responded with mock jealousy.

Donavin chuckled. "I really enjoyed you. I hope we can do it again really soon."

"As a matter of fact we can. How does Friday night sound? Bring J.R. and Adam, and I'll bring two of my girls."

"What do you have in mind?"

"I was thinking that we could hit up Lola's. It's a nice little spot on West Twenty-second Street where they have live music."

"Are your friends cute, Jas? J.R. and Spoon will bitch and moan to me if they're not."

"I think you know one of them. Do you remember Stacia Jones from school?"

"Yeah, she graduated two years ago and was an econ major, if I recall correctly. I'm just asking because the fellas are a little picky. Well, at least Spoon is . . . a little bit."

"And I'm sure they'll like Carmen. She's short, Puerto Rican, and has a big chest and a big butt. That's what most brothers like, right?"

Donavin laughed, thinking that with those stats Carmen would probably have J.R. wide open. "Yeah, bruthas do like the curves. Sounds like a plan then. My boys will definitely be up for it."

"So, do you think you'll be *up* for it?" Jasmine purred.

"You are such the tease, Jasmine. Don't speak about it, be about it."

"Just playing again. But since I have you on the phone, I want to talk to you about last night. I mean I usually don't have men stay over on the first date. I don't want you to think I'm that way."

"I don't. On the real. I'm feeling you, Jasmine. I thought that last night was very special. I think that the whole evening was something neither of us expected."

"No doubt. That doesn't happen very often that I let somebody get so close so soon."

"I say we just take things as they come and see how it goes."

"Listen, I know you have another year left in school and you're going to want to enjoy your last year to the fullest. I want you to understand that I'm not gonna try and hold you down."

"You're new to New York, aren't you?"

"Yeah, I'm from Richmond. Why do you ask?"

"So you'll be meeting new people and doing your thing as well. I think we should just kick it and see what happens. Deal?"

"Deal. So does seven on Friday work for you guys?"

"We'll see y'all then."

"Donavin, for some reason I trust you. I just thought you should know that."

Puzzled, Donavin said, "Um . . . thanks, Jas. I'll see you Friday."

"Yes, you will, Brown Eyes."

Donavin was confused by what just happened. *What the hell does "I trust you" mean? Is she playing some sort of game?*

He finally hung up the phone but he couldn't shake his thoughts. He kept thinking about how much they had connected. Even though they didn't make love, he didn't feel like anything was missing from the night they had shared. He knew that circumstances would make it difficult for them, but something deep down was telling him to give it a try.

CHAPTER
SIX

Friday after work Donavin and crew met up at the Columbia dorm room to prepare for their evening out.

J.R. stopped ironing his shirt. "What do deez friends look like? Fine girls usually travel wit' ugly broads to push dey own stock up. I ain't spendin' no money on no crazy chickenhead-lookin' broads."

Donavin was exasperated. "You guys remember Stacia Jones from Stratford? Tall high-yellow female with a high booty? She's an Epsilon."

Spoon remembered her immediately. "Certainly. I believe she graduated the year before last. Very innocent on the outside, but quite the wildcat behind closed doors, I understand. I'll take that assignment."

"The other one I heard is a nice Puerto Rican shorty. I heard she's P.H.A.T.—Pretty Hot And Tantalizing."

"Man!" J.R. exclaimed. "I been wantin' to hit a Puerto Rican broad all summa, dawg. Dat one's mine. I'm wit' it. Hoodie hoo! I'm gon' beat it up so big!"

Donavin rolled his eyes as he tucked his shirt into his slacks. "Slow your roll, playboy. These aren't college girls. These are women. Just play it cool."

Spoon was engrossed with checking his reflection in the mirror but found a moment to say, "I concur, J.R. Let's just get dressed and meet these young ladies so we can give them an evening they'll be hard-pressed to forget."

"I don't know what da hell y'all talkin 'bout. I'm a southern playa. Matter o' fact, I'm playerific. Better yet, make dat macktastic. I git excited 'bout hittin' deez broads off. Mark my words, dat Puerto Rican girl is gon' be callin' me papi by da end of da night! Guaranteed!"

Spoon paid absolutely no attention to J.R.'s comments as he eyed himself once more. "It should really be a crime for one man to look this damn good."

"Do you guys think this outfit looks cute?" Jasmine asked, stepping into her living room to model for Stacia and Carmen. She was wearing a black silk and rayon blend miniskirt with a red halter-top and black open-toed high-heeled shoes.

"Ay mami, you are muy caliente. That looks fly as hell. The short skirt and that skimpy top make you look like a little hoochie momma, but you look good."

"Carm, you always know just what to say," Jasmine answered sarcastically.

"I don't know what you're concerned about," Stacia said, interjecting her two cents. "You're gonna get some tonight regardless of what you've got on."

"Whateva, boo," Jasmine said, flipping Stacia the bird. "Don't hate because he's fine and he's trying to holler at me."

"Noboby's hating you, ma. Hell, I hope he gives it to you real good so you can stop being so uptight."

"Oh, stop it. You two bitches are always so catty." Carmen threw her hands in the air then grabbed her purse. "Will y'all come on already!"

Excitement began to build as the three women set out for Lola's, anxious to meet up with the guys. It was kind of a game—their team being the underdog and the BDP as the defending champion. They drew confidence when they stepped onto the street from the many votes of approval from passing motorists who beeped their horns at them.

The women arrived at Lola's five minutes early. They moved past the bar area, sat down at a table for six, and placed their drink orders. Little did they know that they were being watched from across the street where Donavin and company hid behind a parked U-Haul truck.

"Looks like our prey has arrived and is ready to be acquired," Spoon observed. "Let's keep them waiting until about five minutes after the hour and then move in. It's all about power positioning."

Donavin nodded. "Excellent plan, Spoon."

"Did y'all see da ass on dat Puerto Rican broad? I gots to hit dat. Dis ain't a game now!"

The BDP hung out inconspicuously across the street for ten more minutes and then decided to move in. They walked in one after the other, turning the heads of all the women in the room—including their dates. Confidence oozed from their pores as they walked toward the table. When Donavin saw Jasmine, he took the lead and went over to her.

Donavin winked at her and gave her the BDP smile. "Hey, you." He wrapped his hand around her waist and gave her a squeeze. As her perfume filled his nostrils again, he realized how much he'd missed her.

"Hey, yourself. Don't you guys look like a trio of cover models."

Stacia pretended to clear her throat to remind Jasmine to do proper introductions.

"Sorry, I didn't mean to be rude. These are my friends Stacia

Jones and Carmen Gutierrez."

Donavin also made introductions. "J.R. James and Adam Witherspoon."

Everyone shook hands and exchanged pleasantries. The game was now in motion and the BDP set out to take control of the pawns. J.R. sat next to Carmen, Spoon next to Stacia, and Donavin next to Jasmine. The BDP wasted no time laying down game like no one else was even sitting there. It was as if three individual couples unknown to each other were sitting at the table.

Donavin gazed into Jasmine's eyes. "It looks like our friends have taken a liking to each other."

"I'd say. I'm glad. But enough about them, how are you, Brown Eyes?"

"I'm cool. This was a great idea. You look absolutely breath-taking."

"Stop it." She grinned, enjoying the compliment. "Well, never mind. Tell me more."

"Your hair, your eyes, mmm, those legs. You make me wanna—"

"Wanna what?" Jasmine shot back.

"Be creative and use your imagination."

They held hands underneath the table and began to gently stroke each other's fingers.

Jasmine drew closer to Donavin and whispered, "I've missed you, Brown Eyes. You should've seen the way all these women were gawking at you guys when you came in."

"We did. We loved it. But don't act innocent. We saw the fellas watching you all pretty hard, too. Your friends are both very attrac-tive. Spoon and J.R. seem to be most pleased."

"Shit, Stace and Carm seem to be most pleased."

"Look, Baby Girl, our friends seem to be doing their thing. I don't think it would be a bad idea for us to separate from them at some point in the evening."

"You sure cut to the chase, don't you? I'm feeling you, though. We'll just have to look for our window of opportunity and slip out."

"Let's bounce in like an hour or so."

"Cool."

Donavin smiled and snuggled into Jasmine's neck. She playfully giggled as his lips tickled her nape and discreetly peeked over to see how Stacia was faring with pretty Spoon.

"Adam, you look all grown up now." Stacia reached over and ran her manicured hand down the length of his arm from shoulder to fingertip.

"I've been taking my vitamins. And please, call me Spoon."

"What have you been up to this summer?"

"A little of this, a little of that."

"What does 'a little of this' and 'a little of that' consist of?"

"You know, just hitting up a party here and there and getting into various adventures with these two characters." He nodded toward J.R. and Donavin.

"I can only imagine. So, what do you do besides get into parties and adventures? There's *so* much to see and do in the city." Stacia licked her lips to emphasize her point.

Sensing her suggestive body language, Spoon played it off like he wasn't fazed. "I like to read and go to museums," he said nonchalantly.

"Really? I absolutely love the Museum of Modern Art. Have you been this season?"

"Absolutely. The Jackie Onassis exhibit was truly fascinating."

Stacia found herself becoming increasingly attracted to Spoon. By his mannerisms and the way he spoke, she could tell that he was a cocky bastard. But he was a fine and cultured cocky bastard. "Wow, I never figured you for an art lover."

"I'm sure there are lots of things you don't know about me."

"Like what?" Stacia raised an eyebrow.

"Well, it's kind of loud in here. Why don't we go somewhere and talk in a quieter setting?" Spoon suggested, much to Stacia's delight.

"Sure, but let's just wait a little while to keep up appearances."

"I'm sure they'll hardly even notice." They shared a conspiratorial chuckle and took a sip of their beverages. Stacia looked over her apple martini across the table at Carmen, who was being wooed.

"I've never met anyone from New Orleans," Carmen said, sizing J.R. up. "I've always wanted to go to Mardi Gras, though."

"No doubt, girl. We git down in da bayou."

"How do you like New York?"

"Dis city is so big and unfriendly. I'm useta southern hospitality. Y'all so mean up here."

"I'm not mean and I'm from here." Carmen batted her eyelashes in an exaggerated manner.

J.R. laughed at her antics. "Maybe you da exception. But fuh real, I'm 'bout ready to go back to Atlanta so I can listen to some Hot Boys, Trick Daddy, and Master P. I'm tired of all dis east coast hip hop. Talkin' 'bout all da guns dey got and shit like dat. I like music 'bout ridin' and pimpin'. Dat down south ghetto music. Dat's what I like. In dis city, you can't hardly even drive around. Here we keep our cars in garages all da time. I just wanna ride out to some music dat makes you wanna back dat ass up. Is dat so wrong?"

Carmen laughed. "Stop it, papi! You're making my drink come out of my nose."

J.R. sat up on full alert. There was something very sexy to him about a Latina calling him papi, especially this Latina. He immediately realized he needed to get her isolated from her friends so he could work his mojo.

"Have you seen a lot of New York?" Carmen asked once she regained her composure.

"Guaranteed I have not. I've just hit up da parties wit' deez two fools. Dey ain't showed me nothin' but da inside o' clubs 'n bars.

Deez Negroes have been hella unhospicultural in showin' me da sights. You like my new word?"

"You are so crazy. Hmm." Carmen thought for a moment. "Do you like salsa music, J.R.?"

J.R. pretended that he knew a little about the genre and said, "Fuh sho. Ricky Martin is like off da hook. 'La Loca Vida' is da hotness!"

"That's 'La Vida Loca', silly! But that's not what I'm talking about. I mean real Latin music. You know like Tito Puente and Celia Cruz. We should go salsa dancing sometime. I think you'd like it. You look like you can move." Carmen parted her lips and looked at J.R. seductively.

J.R. recognized his easy way in. "What's up on right now, girl?"

They both grinned at one another and J.R. moved his hand to Carmen's thigh. He could tell by the way she flirted that she liked him, and he wanted to waste no time in capitalizing on the opportunity.

"We can't just leave our friends," Carmen protested.

J.R. gestured toward Donavin and Spoon who were paying him no mind. "Deez ol' ashy Negroes look like dey doin' jus' fine, and yo' girlfriends look to be enjoyin' demselves as well. I wanna see what's up on dat Tito Cruz." J.R. winked and nudged closer to Carmen.

She didn't bother correcting him. "Aight, papi. Let's just grab a few more drinks and then make a graceful exit." Carmen winked and nudged back.

Ignoring Carmen, J.R. rose to his feet. "I feel like dancin', y'all. But I ain't tryna shake my ass like normal. I wanna do some salsa dancin'." J.R. shook his shoulders rapidly to an imaginary beat.

Donavin and Spoon responded in unison, "*Salsa dancing?*" Jasmine and Stacia looked puzzled as well.

"You ol' ashy Negroes heard me. I'm tryna listen to some Pito Tuente."

"Tito Puente, papi!"

"Yeah, what she said." J.R. gestured toward Carmen.

"The only thing you know about salsa is that it tastes good with tortilla chips," Donavin joked.

"Yeah, man, what's your favorite brand? Ortega? Old El Paso?" Spoon said amidst a chorus of laughter.

"Well, since y'all sound less dan enthusiastic, me and Carmen are jus' gon' go and do our own thang. Minus y'all haters."

Spoon gave J.R. a wicked smile and said, "Have a good time, brother."

Spoon and J.R. locked eyes and Spoon knew exactly what J.R. was thinking. Now it was time to separate, isolate, then penetrate.

"Stacia." Spoon turned his attention toward her. "Let's dip downtown to the Blue Note. It's a mellow little spot. You like jazz?"

"That sounds good. I'm game."

Spoon and Stacia followed J.R. and Carmen out of Lola's, leaving Jasmine and Donavin alone.

"Jas, looks like we've been deserted. Guess we didn't need to sneak out after all."

"It certainly seems that way."

"Let's make some plans of our own," Donavin whispered into her ear as he nibbled on her lobe.

Jasmine closed her eyes at the sensation she felt. "Yeah, let's."

Jasmine and Donavin both knew they wanted a more private gathering so they hailed a cab back to her place. They took the journey up to the second floor once again with Jasmine leading Donavin by the hand.

"Looks like we're here," Jasmine said.

"Sure does." Donavin closed and locked the door behind them. "Why don't you pop in some relaxing music?"

"Like some Sade or Maxwell?"

"Yeah, that's what's up."

Donavin stood to the side while Jasmine randomly programmed a few CDs. She returned to him and kissed him as the music started to play. They swayed in time to the rhythm.

Before too long, Jasmine took Donavin by the hand and led him back to her bedroom. "Make yourself comfortable while I freshen up."

She left him in the middle of her room and disappeared into the bathroom. Donavin grew increasingly optimistic about his chances. He got on the floor and did fifty quick push-ups to make his muscles look bigger. He stripped down to his boxers and climbed into the bed.

Within minutes Jasmine reappeared with a Victoria's Secret black lace bra and a matching thong. She walked over to the window and opened the mini-blinds, which let in the perfect amount of moonlight. She went to another corner of the room and retrieved a bottle from her dresser.

"What's that?" Donavin asked as she straddled him.

"It's Kama Sutra body oil."

Jasmine uncapped the bottle and poured some oil in her palms. She rubbed her hands together to warm the oil then slid her hands down the length of his chest and stomach, staring at him as she kneaded his flesh. Donavin closed his eyes and moaned from the intensity of her touch.

Jasmine stopped abruptly and lay her hands on his stomach. "What do you think of me, Brown Eyes?"

Donavin felt distracted by her question. He was perfectly happy just getting the massage, but she had to go starting a conversation. The nerve of her.

"Um . . . you know I really like you a lot. I feel like we click."

"Click as in you can just get some before you go back to school and that'll be it?"

"No, not at all. Jas, what's the matter?"

"Nothing's the matter. I just have questions about your intentions toward me, that's all. I mean, what's going on in that dome of yours?"

"Look, Baby Girl, you've probably heard a ton of bad things about me, but I want you to decide for yourself if you want to listen to what other people say or what this says." Donavin took one of her hands and placed it on his chest over his heart. "I don't have a crystal ball that can see into the future to tell you what's gonna happen. All I know is the here and now. And right here and right now there are no guarantees, no commitments. The only thing we can do is see where whatever this is leads us." Donavin sat up and pulled her closer to him.

"I'm not trying to spoil the mood. I just want us to be on the same page."

"You aren't. I think that your question was perfectly valid." Donavin stroked her cheek, pushing her hair out of her eyes.

"I just want you to know that I already really like you a lot, and I just don't want you to fuck me over. I just want you to be honest with me. No more, no less."

"I respect that. I promise to be honest with you."

"So why do I feel like I'm gonna get played? I saw how you and your friends gamed us tonight. The old divide and conquer trick."

Donavin laughed uneasily, realizing that the BDP had been caught in the act. "Well, your girlfriends looked like willing participants to me. I suppose that at times getting women has been a game to us. I just hope you don't think that I'm trying to play games with you, though."

"How can I be sure?"

"You can't. As I said before, there are no guarantees. You'll just have to have a little faith in me."

Jasmine pondered Donavin's statement then replied, "Fair enough. So, let's say we were to finish what we started and I go ahead and give you a night of butt-naked ecstasy like you've never known?"

"I suppose I'd say thanks." Donavin smiled and they both laughed.

Jasmine put her arms around him and kissed his cheek. She felt more comfortable now with things out in the open. She also respected the fact that Donavin had been honest instead of saying exactly what she wanted to hear. She expected him to say some lovey dovey shit to try and get the drawers, which would have been her cue to put him out, but the fact that he kept it real with her impressed her.

"Hold on a second, Brown Eyes."

Jasmine climbed off of him and walked back into the living room. Moments later she returned and the sounds of Stevie Wonder's classic "Ribbon in the Sky" filled the air.

"Like Stevie, Brown Eyes?"

"A musical genius, girl. Now, why don't you climb into this bed and finish that massage you started?"

Donavin rolled over onto his stomach and Jasmine climbed on top of him again. She began to rub his shoulders, and he fell back into his relaxed state from before. She let her fingers explore the rest of his back and arms. Donavin's breathing slowed as her hands gently moved down his spine.

Jasmine whispered, "You're not falling asleep on me, are you?"

"Never that, Jas. No need to stop. Keep going."

Jasmine reached over to the nightstand to get more Kama Sutra oil. She unscrewed the cap and began to pour more into her hands. The bottle slipped and half of its contents spilled onto Donavin's underwear.

Jasmine gasped. "Oh my God! Donavin, I'm so sorry!"

"It's okay, Baby Girl. Here, why don't you go ahead and take them off?"

"Uh . . . okay."

Jasmine took his boxers by the waistband and eased them off. He lay there nude. She struggled to keep her cool as she resumed the massage. She spread oil on his cheeks and worked her way down his legs to the tips of his toes.

"Mmm . . . that feels so good. Can I turn over now?" Donavin innocently asked.

"Uh . . . okay."

Donavin turned over onto his back. His erect penis beckoned to Jasmine's widened eyes.

"Come here," Donavin said as he patted the space on the bed next to him. Jasmine lay down in silence. "Jasmine, meet Little Donavin. Little Donavin, meet Jasmine."

Jasmine laughed.

"He says he's very pleased to meet you."

She reached down to stroke Donavin. "And I'm very pleased to meet him, though he's not very little."

Donavin laughed and positioned himself on top of her. Only her bra and thong separated them. "He wants to know if he can get a little closer to you." He kissed her all over her face and made his way to her neck in an effort to convince her. He felt her body acquiesce as she wrapped both legs around his waist.

Yes! I'm about to get it. Whew! I thought I was losing my touch.

"Oh, Donavin . . . oh, Donavin . . ." Jasmine panted.

"Yes, Jasmine . . . yes."

"Oh, Donavin . . . I . . . I just can't! The time isn't right."

Donavin stopped moving and propped himself up on his arms. "Baby Girl, we got Stevie singing, we got the oils glistening, we got the moonlight beaming, and there ain't but two pieces of cloth between me and you. How much righter can it get?"

"I just think that we'll enjoy it more and it'll be more special if we wait. Yeah, let's wait." Jasmine resolved herself to her decision.

Donavin clenched his teeth. "Wait? Wait?" Then his senses kicked in. *Don't ever beg. That's conduct unbecoming a player.*

He rolled off of her stiffly and said, "Sure, Jasmine. Yeah, let's wait. Let's just get some rest."

"Actually, I'm really horny right now, and I think I'll be too tempted with you here. Can you stay with Spoon and J.R. tonight?"

"You're kicking me out?"

"Please, it's not like that. I just need a little time."

Donavin was really pissed off, but he didn't let it show. He replied in an even tone, "Well, I guess I'll be on my way then."

Donavin put on his clothes—minus the greasy drawers—and began walking toward the door. He dialed a number on his cell phone.

"Hey, J.R., do you fellas mind if I crash?"

"No problem, playa. Did you hit it?"

Donavin ignored the question. "I'll be through in a little while." He hung up the phone and turned his attention to Jasmine. "Well, I guess I'll holler at you."

"Don't be like that, Brown Eyes. If you really like me like you say you do, you'll wait. I promise that it'll be worth it."

She grabbed him by the shirt and gave him a long goodbye kiss. The two hugged, then Donavin headed to Manhattan. He was absolutely stunned by what had just happened. She was ready, he was ready, and now he was out the door. He hoped that neither of his friends got some because he dreaded their ridicule.

He caught a cab and made it to Columbia University shortly after three in the morning. He was greeted by the sound of Missy Elliot's "Get Ur Freak On" with Spoon and J.R. drinking what seemed to be congratulatory toasts. J.R. bounced to the music as he drank.

Spoon greeted him at the door. "Shall we pour you a glass of Cristal in celebration? And why is your underwear in your hand and not on your behind?"

"Long story. I'll skip the fucking champagne." Donavin stormed past Spoon and flopped down on their couch.

J.R. was astonished. "Playboy! At Lola's dat broad looked like she wanted you so big. You ain't lay no smackdown?"

"Sure didn't. My game must really be slippin'. Picture this. She's got a thong on, bodies are all oiled up, Stevie Wonder's playing in the background, and she starts with this 'let's wait' bullshit." Donavin put his hands to his temple and shook his head. "This has never happened to me before, fellas. Then she kicked me out because she said that she was too tempted. I don't believe this shit! If I don't hit the first time, I always hit the second. This is fucking me up. Anyway, don't tell me you two jokers got some."

J.R. and Spoon smiled at each other and J.R. began. "I could tell you dat we didn't hit, but I would clearly be lyin'. Dawg, we beat it up so big!"

"Details, details. Even though I'm disappointed, I can live through y'all."

"Okay, playboy, check dis out. First me and Carmen went to da Copacabana on Fifty-seventh Street. Guaranteed I don't like no salsa music, but whateva. Dawg, dey had some of da finest breezies walkin' dis earth up in dat joint. Fine ass Puerto Rican, Dominican, and Cuban breezies jus' profilin' and lookin' good. Damn, I hate y'all fuh neva takin' me dere, but I digress. Y'all, I got dat broad so drunk. She started grabbin' on my ass on da dance floor and den she grabbed my ding-a-ling."

Donavin and Spoon erupted with laughter at J.R.'s knack for storytelling.

"After dat I was like 'Check, please! Time to beat it up.' We took a cab back to her place and dat broad tackled me like a man and shit. Shoot, I was 'bout to pop her in da mouth, but I chilled 'cause I realized dat she was jus' a little anxious to get at dat chocolate playboy named J.R. James. Den I jus' picked her up, threw her over my shoulder, and took it to da bedroom. Dat girl took off all of her clothes and da body was off da hook! Dat broad is in da same category as Jennifer Lopez. Guaranteed! I wasted no time and stripped, too. Den she went platinum on me."

Puzzled, Spoon and Donavin looked at each other and Donavin said, "What the hell do you mean 'she went platinum'?"

"I mean she got on da mic. I got some skully. You know, some brain." J.R. then began to make obscene gestures to simulate oral sex. "I was 'bout to bust, but I made her stop so I could give it a hearty ass beat. I flipped her onto her stomach and da next thing I know I'm makin' dat breezie bite da pillows fuh real. Dat man Jay-Z made dat song 'Big Pimpin'' 'bout me."

"Stop lying!" Donavin looked at J.R. incredulously.

"My momma ain't raise no fibber. Man, she started callin' me papi and shit. It was off da damn hook!"

Donavin turned to Spoon. "I don't know if you can top that, but let's hear it."

"My experience was rather delightful. After Lola's, we went to listen to some jazz at the Blue Note. Man, they had this sax player that was just hitting these notes—"

"Spoon!" J.R. interrupted him. "You are seriously borin' me right now. Git to da coochie, man! Damn!"

"Yeah, Spoon. It's late as hell and a brother is getting tired."

"If you two would demonstrate some patience. I'm getting to it. Anyway, she told me that she had the CD to the opera *Carmina Burana*. I was naturally fascinated and suggested that we go to her place and check it out."

J.R. was now interested again. "Finally, Spoon! Git on wit' it. Shit!"

"We got to her tastefully decorated apartment in Harlem. First, we listened to the CD. It was moving, to say the least. Quite a spectacular piece of work. We sat in her living room sipping on some red wine and then we began to kiss to 'O Fortuna'. For you two cretins, that would be the original piece of music behind 'Hate Me Now' by Nas and Puffy or P. Diddy, whichever you choose to call him. The kiss itself was orgasmic. The music heightened the sexual tension, and I began to slowly kiss her nape."

"Then what?" Donavin asked, exasperated.

"I must have hit her spot because then we just started going at it. She practically jumped on me, but I slowed her down to let her know who was in control. I took her into her bedroom and undressed her. Then I turned the light on and just looked at her body. She had the roundest breasts with these succulent nipples, a six pack to rival mine, and a wonderful pair of muscular legs."

"Yeah, dawg, she beige like you, too. Y'all can have some transparent ass kids."

Spoon continued, ignoring J.R. "Now, we're both naked, tipsy, and the opera music is playing in the background. Then I go to get a condom. You do know what one of those is, don't you, J.R.? Con-dom?"

"I always strap up. I just cut da fat when I tell a story. Yo' long-winded ass talkin' 'bout operas and shit."

"Anyway, I was about to strap up, as you so eloquently put it, when, much like your sweet Carmen, she started to do something outstanding with her mouth. I was about to have a special moment, but I had to lay some smackdown."

Spoon and J.R. gave each other a high-five.

"So, we start doing it and our bodies are just grinding against each other. Just in and out. Then she got on top and she just started shifting her hips and going crazy. She went from slow, to medium, to light speed, to ludicrous speed. I think we came at the same time. Then we exchanged numbers and I dipped out."

"I knew Stacia was a freak, but damn. I'm really mad that you two clowns hit both of those chicks and you knew them both for a total of four hours. I feel like a loser for real."

Spoon encouraged his friend. "Playboy, don't talk like that. You have been an inspiration to both of us over the last three years. We don't leave for Atlanta until Wednesday. You still have a few days to accomplish your mission. If the tables were turned, you would've gotten with Stacia or Carmen and one of us would be upset about not getting any. Don't give up, my friend. If you get it before Wednesday, it just makes your legend that much greater."

"Yeah, dawg! Spoon is right. You done hit a lot of broads. Law of averages says dat at some point you gots to lose. Or at least wait a while. We won't give you da business too much today. But if you don't hit it by Wednesday . . ."

"I will hit it!" Donavin spoke with confidence. "I'm making this my manifest destiny. I will be victorious, gentleman."

Spoon encouraged Donavin again. "That's the spirit. It's always darkest before the dawn. Speaking of dawn. Good night, my brothers. I need my beauty sleep."

CHAPTER SEVEN

On Saturday afternoon Donavin scraped himself up and took a bus back to New Jersey. During the entire ride home he had one thing on his mind—getting some from Jasmine. Donavin walked into his parent's house and smelled a pleasing aroma, briefly taking his mind off of Operation Jasmine.

"Hey, Momma, what's up?" Donavin greeted his mother in the kitchen preparing lunch.

"Hey, baby, you look tired. Late night?"

"Yeah, I hung out with my friend, Jasmine, last night."

"A new girl, huh? I knew there had to be a reason why you've been out so much lately. Do you like her for the right reasons?"

Donavin sat down at the table behind her. "I always look for young ladies of substance. You know that."

Mrs. Jackson scrunched up her nose and sucked her teeth. "Boy, I told you about using those lines on me. Leave that stuff in the street. So, tell me about her."

"Her name is Jasmine and she's a management consultant. She graduated from Stratford in May. She's kinda cool, though. Might be the settle-down piece."

"'The settle-down piece'? Can I have that in English, please?"

"Sorry," Donavin rethought his speech and said, "I think she may be girlfriend material."

"Wow, she must be something for you to say that. Keep me post—" She began to cough profusely in front of the stove.

"Momma!" Donavin rushed to her side. "Are you okay?"

Catching her breath, she said, "Pour me a glass of water, Donny."

He did as she asked and watched her take small sips.

Mrs. Jackson held her hand against her stomach. "I've been fighting this cold lately. I think I need to lie down."

"Momma, are you sure you're okay?" Donavin said with concern in his eyes.

"Yeah, baby." She lightly rubbed his cheek. "Your father is taking a nap upstairs. I'll just go up and join him."

"All right, Momma."

Mrs. Jackson walked slowly up the stairs to the east wing of the house with Donavin holding her hand.

"You had a late night, sweetie. Go and get some rest."

"You do the same." He kissed her on the cheek and headed to his room, which was in the west wing.

Donavin's room featured a forty-inch LCD flat screen television, a twenty-gallon fish tank that was part of the wall, and a state-of-the-art Sony sound system. As he lay on his king-size bed, he went through every possible scenario in his BDP playbook but came up empty. He had to make it happen with Jasmine. He just had to figure out how. He rested until the early evening and then he decided to call Jasmine.

"What's up, Baby Girl?"

"Hey, Brown Eyes."

"How're you doing?"

"A little tired, but I'm making it. You know our friends are freaks, right?"

Donavin laughed. "You heard, huh?"

"Ugh! Did I! Both Carmen and Stacia called me this morning and informed me of their pornographic episodes. Your friends get high marks. Are you as good?"

"Only one way to find out."

"How is that?"

"Practice."

Jasmine purred like Eartha Kitt. "What kind of practice are you talking about?"

"Why don't we hook up Monday after work and I'll show you what I mean."

"Isn't that your last day at work?"

"Yeah, then we're headed to Atlanta on Wednesday."

"So this is goodbye?"

"Never that. Just a temporary parting. What do you say we make it a Blockbuster night on Monday? I don't feel like sharing you with the rest of the world."

"I can work with that. My place at 7:30?"

"Cool. See you then."

With that, they hung up and both thought Monday would be the day. Each lay awake that night in anticipation of what was to come. Donavin had a now-or-never attitude, and he was definitely partial to now as opposed to never. Jasmine knew in her heart that she wanted to fully give herself to him. She was growing tired of her own games.

CHAPTER EIGHT

Monday was devoted mainly to housekeeping issues at work for Donavin. He went through several rounds of exit interviews for his internship, but his mind was preoccupied with after-work pursuits. At 4:30, he was pleasantly surprised by a party thrown in his honor at which he was extended an offer to return to Proctor and Proctor after the successful completion of his senior year. He took this as a good omen. After doing the corporate thing with his co-workers, he focused on the real task at hand.

He arrived at Jasmine's on time, and she buzzed him up without asking who it was. Jasmine answered the door wearing tight khaki capri pants and a pink button-down shirt with three buttons undone. The shirt was tied at her waist to give Donavin a sneak peek at her flat stomach. She wore light makeup, and her hair was pinned up with a few sexy tendrils framing her face and neck.

"Baby Girl, you look lovely." Donavin looked her over, then hugged her and handed her a bottle of Alizé.

"Thanks, Brown Eyes. Alizé is my favorite. Good thinking."

He walked in and sat down on the couch. Instantly he smelled the aroma of home cooking. "Whatcha got cookin', girl?"

"Oh, not much. Just some fried chicken, mashed potatoes, macaroni and cheese, steamed vegetables, and homemade biscuits. You like?"

"*Damn.* I do."

"So, how was your last day? Must feel good to be free?"

"Yes, it does, especially when you get a job offer."

"That's great! That means this is a celebratory dinner. Let's eat."

The two went to the kitchen and fixed themselves plates of what Jasmine had prepared. It tasted as good as it smelled, and Donavin was impressed with her culinary expertise.

"Damn, you hooked this food up!" Donavin leaned back and patted his stomach.

"Thanks. I only do this for special company."

"I'm special?"

"Don't you feel special?"

Donavin reached across the table to caress Jasmine's hand. "I do now."

"Dance with me."

Jasmine stood from the table, took him by the hand, and guided him toward the living room. She put in a CD and the sounds of "Moments in Love" came through the speakers. Then she dimmed the lights and lit a three-wick candle. She returned to Donavin and wrapped her arms around his neck. They began to sway in rhythmic motion. In each other's arms, everything and nothing was said. They let the melody of the music do all of the talking for them.

Donavin gently massaged Jasmine's cheek with his right hand and began to softly kiss the left side of her face. Jasmine closed her eyes tightly as a feeling of ecstasy came over her.

"What about the movie?" she whispered.

Donavin whispered back, "We'll watch it next time." He moved to her mouth and enveloped her lips with his. Their tongues danced to the rhythm as well. Donavin knew that Jasmine could feel his erection through his pants. He pulled away from her kiss. Jasmine wrinkled her eyebrows.

"What's wr—"

Donavin silenced her when he picked her up in his arms and marched toward her bedroom. He lay her down on the bed and began to undress her.

"Wait a second."

Damn! Not again!

"I know you've probably done it with a lot of girls, but—"

"Look, I told you—"

"No, no, what I'm saying is that I don't want you to just do it. I want you to make love to me, Donavin. Now."

Donavin hesitated because he just knew that she was going to put the brakes on again. He knew exactly what she was talking about in regard to making love as opposed to just having sex. He knew that this night was special and that she deserved to be made love to.

He began to undress her and it was as if he was seeing her for the first time. Her body was soft and moist with a hint of perspiration. He then massaged her breasts gently and nibbled on her nipples. Jasmine moaned as she held him in her bosom, and she stroked his head in a circular motion. Donavin then moved in between her breasts and slowly slid his tongue down to her stomach, then inside her belly button.

"Oh my God." She closed her eyes in anticipation of what was to come.

Donavin then kissed her thighs and teased her by blowing on her moistening slit.

"Don't make me beg, Donavin." She felt powerless as his aura consumed her and their spirits became intertwined.

He gave in to her and his tongue began to explore her most sensitive of areas.

"Oh! Oh!" She gripped the sheets as ecstasy came over her. Donavin kissed his way back up her stomach to her breasts, then to her lips.

"Lay back," Jasmine said. Jasmine and Donavin switched positions. She pressed her hands against his chest and straddled him. She put her tongue in his ear and then sucked his earlobes.

"Mmm." Donavin moaned as she played with his spot.

Jasmine then explored his neck and gently massaged his chest. Then she went south on him, lightly kissing his abdomen until she came to his pulsing erection. She ran her tongue up and down his shaft and then she took him into her mouth.

"Oh . . . shit!" It was Donavin's turn to make holes in the sheets. She orally pleased him like he had never been pleased. She then kissed her way back north and whispered in his ear.

"Make love to me, Donavin."

They took the necessary precaution and began a lovemaking feast unlike any that either had ever experienced. They matched each other stroke for stroke and made love for hours. Although Donavin was very experienced in affairs of the bedroom he had never known such pleasure. He'd had lots of sex, but he had never made love to a woman before. What really blew his mind was that Jasmine made love to him in return. She touched him like she meant it, and she did.

The next morning Donavin awoke to Jasmine gazing at him and stroking his hair.

"Good morning, Baby Girl."

"Good morning, Brown Eyes. Nice performance last night."

"Well, you know . . . what can I say?" Donavin said in his best J.J. Evans impersonation.

Jasmine remained serious. "Was this a one-time event?"

"No, Jas, I really like you. I need you to believe that. We're just in different stages in our lives. We just have to go with the flow and see what happens."

"Gotcha. I feel the same way. We'll go with the flow."

It was total bullshit on both parts. Neither of them wanted to admit that they were both overwhelmed by the night they had shared. They had opened the Pandora's Box of passion, and there was no closing it now.

"What time are you leaving Wednesday?"

"The fellas are coming to my parent's house at about seven in the morning."

"Call me before you leave."

"I will, sweetheart. I will." Donavin leaned over and kissed her forehead.

The two then got out of bed and prepared for the day. After they were dressed they stood for a few minutes at her front door just looking at one another and holding hands.

"I'll miss you, Brown Eyes."

"Me, too."

"You know we have some visits to schedule."

"True that. I haven't seen nearly as much of you as I need to."

Jasmine melted inside but didn't show it. They shared a long kiss and embrace, then headed toward the door. Once outside, they went their separate ways.

CHAPTER
NINE

"Mmm. Those eggs and pancakes smell so good, Momma. I can't wait!" Donavin rubbed his stomach in anticipation.

"My boy needs a good breakfast for that long drive. If you had gone to Rutgers or Columbia, you could have eaten like this all the time."

"I needed to go out and establish my own identity. Wouldn't have been able to do that very well with you teaching at Columbia. As far as Rutgers, it's in New Brunswick, New Jersey. Need I say more? Besides, you went to Stratford."

"I'm just saying that it would be nice for you to be around more."

"Don't worry about that. Next year when I'm doing the Wall Street thing, we'll have plenty of time to hang out."

"My little boy is about to graduate. Doesn't seem like it was that long ago when I was in school or got together with your father during senior year."

"Good morning." Donavin Sr. sauntered down the stairs in his forest green bathrobe with his initials monogrammed on the lapel. He walked over to Mrs. Jackson and kissed her cheek. "I remember when you stopped kidding yourself and finally realized that I was the one."

"Oh, please." Mrs. Jackson rolled her eyes and continued cooking.

"Let me tell you the story right quick, Donavin." Mr. Jackson sat at the head of the kitchen table and leaned back as he reminisced.

"Why do I feel like one of the Cosby kids about to hear one of Heathcliff Huxtable's long-winded stories?" Donavin asked, laughing.

"Hey, respect your elders, boy. Okay, it was right around Valentine's Day in 1976. No, I mean 1977. That's right. It was 1977 when we graduated from school. It was the day before Valentine's Day 1977. I had been diggin' your momma for a long time, but she wasn't giving me any play. Then there was this guy. If I remember correctly, his name was Philip. Philip Edwins. Philip Edgars. Some crap. Whatever his name was he was a real loser. He was a Beta, too, and we just didn't get along for whatever reason."

"Ooh," Donavin interjected. "Betas are the worst!"

"I wonder what that fool is doing now? Anyway, I'm in the cafeteria and he comes up to me and tells me how I had better leave your mom alone and how he was going to take her out for Valentine's Day. I was sitting there with a few of my boys, so I had to correct him quickly. Then we started playing the dozens and I talked about him, his momma, and his daddy. I was cracking myself up as I talked about his tired behind. So now there's a big crowd and your mother approaches, and I assume she asked someone in the crowd what the argument was about. She pushes her way to where me and Philip were standing and she lets us have it."

"You deserved it," Mrs. Jackson said. "The both of you were acting like I was some sort of carnival prize to be won. Donny, always treat a woman with respect and kindness. Don't try the caveman approach of beating your chest and telling everyone else but the girl how you feel."

70

"I'll continue. She comes up to us and tells us that she's not try-ing to go out with either one of us and that we can feel free to leave her out of our conversation from then on. Then she snapped her fingers and switched her hips from side to side. She thought she was just that fine with those cute little dimples she had."

"That I *still* have, thank you." Mrs. Jackson set breakfast in front of Donavin and Mr. Jackson. She then sat on Mr. Jackson's lap and gently kissed his temple as he continued the story.

"Donavin, Philip got so mad that he stormed out of the cafete-ria almost in tears. My boys had jokes for hours. But I wasn't deterred. That just meant that I had to up the ante. The next day they were crossing a new line of Betas. No, it was like early evening. That's right. All the Betas were in the Quad hootin', hollerin', and steppin' when, much to their surprise, they saw a propeller plane fly low overhead. I waited in my Mustang in the parking lot of Gaines Hall where your mother lived. I remember perfectly—on the second floor in 209. I had a tuxedo on, too. I was too clean, boy. No half-stepping."

Donavin chuckled.

"I knew I had only a few seconds to get her attention so she could see my message attached to the tail of the plane. I threw rocks at her window and when she came to the window she threw an old shoe down and asked me what the hell I was doing. I told her to look up and she did just in time to see the propeller plane with the mes-sage *Miss Vanessa Clark, will you be my Valentine?* trailing the plane. I could tell by her face that I had her. I had my boy standing lookout on the other side of campus at the Beta ceremony. He drove up and told me that the Betas had seen the sign and that they were coming to Gaines Hall to get me. I shouted up to your mother to throw a groovy outfit on and come on so we could go to dinner."

Mrs. Jackson smiled and shook her head. "I already had my hair and makeup done just in case your father did something worthy of my paying attention to him. That old dorm holds a lot of memories. Your father proposed to me on the bench right in front."

"This is wild, Pops. What happened next?"

"I saw a bunch of angry Betas rushing up the hill to Gaines Hall. Your mom was just coming out of her dorm when I grabbed her by the hand and basically threw her in the car. I slipped that bad boy into third and we were outta there. That kid, Philip, hated me after that. The rest is, as they say, history."

The doorbell rang and Donavin got up laughing, expecting to see J.R. and Spoon. The sight of Jasmine greeted his eyes instead.

"Hey, Brown Eyes. I hope you don't mind that I'm surprising you this morning."

Donavin hugged Jasmine, then stepped aside to let her in.

"How did you get here?"

"I borrowed Stacia's car."

"Beautiful and resourceful. Impressive." He held her hand and gazed at her. "Wow, I can't believe you came all the way down here. Before work, no less. I guess you like me a little bit." Donavin winked.

"Maybe. Why don't you come here and find out?" Jasmine pulled him closer and kissed him lightly. He parted her lips with his tongue. "That's enough, Brown Eyes. We don't want your parents to see."

"You're right. Let's save some for later. Come on. You want to meet them? They're in the kitchen." Donavin stroked her cheek. He took her hand and led her through the foyer and living room toward the kitchen.

Jasmine marveled at the mini-mansion. The floors were Italian marble and there seemed to be endless amounts of space. There was also an indoor fountain of which tropical fish were the main inhabitants.

"Looks like we have company, honey. Good morning, young

lady. Donavin Jackson Senior." He stood to introduce himself, extending his hand to Jasmine. Dressed in bedroom attire, Mr. Jackson didn't look like the investment banker turned U.S. congressman that he was, but Jasmine saw clearly where Donavin got his charm and good looks.

"Hello, Congressman Jackson. Jasmine DeRoche."

"If there's one thing my son has, it's certainly taste." He gave her the original old-school BDP smile. "And please, Mr. Jackson is fine."

"Good morning, Jasmine." Mrs. Jackson welcomed her with a hug.

"Good morning, ma'am. How are you this morning?" Jasmine returned.

"Not too well," Mrs. Jackson replied, coughing a bit. "My little boy is leaving me today."

"Mom, don't get yourself all upset."

Mrs. Jackson glanced over at her husband, caught her breath and began to answer. "Oh, I'm fine, Donny. I just miss you when you're not here, that's all." She looked down at the floor and sighed.

Just then the doorbell rang again. Donavin answered it and returned with Spoon and J.R. in tow.

"Good mornin', Jackson family. It's yo' git crunk wake-up call." J.R. greeted everyone as only he could.

Everyone laughed.

"Salutations, all." Spoon shook Mr. Jackson's hand and kissed Mrs. Jackson on the cheek.

"Excuse me, playa." J.R. pushed past Donavin and gave Jasmine a hug and a friendly kiss.

"Hello, J.R." Jasmine rolled her eyes and smiled.

Spoon moved in and kissed Jasmine on both sides of her face. "Sweet Jasmine. Thanks for the . . . um . . . hook-up the other night."

Jasmine smirked. "You're quite welcome."

"Gentlemen," Spoon began, looking pointedly at his friends, "it's almost seven. We'd better get on the road. We've got about twelve hours on the road ahead of us."

"Guaranteed, dawg. Breezies is already anxiously awaitin' my return."

Everyone went outside to the driveway, and Jasmine smothered a giggle at the sight of a line of cars which college students have no business driving—Donavin's Mercedes Benz S Class 430, Spoon's brand new Porsche 911 Carrera 4S, and J.R.'s big, black Lincoln Navigator.

Mr. Jackson stood with the boys in the driveway. "All right, fellas. Be good and study hard. I don't care how many job offers you guys have. By the way, congratulations, Adam, J.R. I understand that you guys got offers as well. School is still the number one priority, though. Don't do anything to prevent yourselves from graduating. I hope I'm understood."

He received a round of "Yes, sirs" and manly hugs from all three of his boys.

Donavin put the last bit of luggage into his trunk. He went over to Jasmine and she kissed him gently. "Have a safe trip, Brown Eyes."

Mrs. Jackson went in the house and came out momentarily with enough food for a small army. She walked over to Donavin, weeping the entire way. "My baby," she said and embraced him near the point of suffocation. "Be safe and take care of each other down there. I love you." She wrapped her arms around him and held on for a few minutes. Her thin body shook with sobs.

At this Donavin began to get a little choked up. "I love you, too, Momma." He wiped a tear from his eye.

Mrs. Jackson released Donavin and went into the house to finish her crying privately.

"You know how your mother is about you, Donny," said Mr.

Jackson, shaking his head. "She'll be okay."

"Befo' we git goin'," J.R. said, rubbing his hands together, "can we see it, Mr. Jackson?"

"See what, J.R.?"

"Oh, come on, Mista J."

"Okay, okay." Mr. Jackson walked toward the garage and flipped the switch to open the last door of the four-car garage. J.R. and Spoon were getting giddy as the door opened slowly.

"Got dang. Dat ride is boss!"

Spoon gasped. "Two hundred sixty-eight pounds of torque. Three hundred seventy-five horsepower. Zero to sixty in four point seven seconds. Often imitated but never duplicated. The ultimate racing machine." Spoon paused for a second and said, "Ferrari F355 Spider," with a rush of air.

"Now, you boys get back down to school so you can graduate and buy one of these for yourselves one day. Drive safely and give a call when you get there."

"Bye, Jas." Donavin winked at her and she blew him a kiss.

With that they hopped into their respective cars, revved their engines, and took off down the street beeping their horns and pissing off all the Jacksons' neighbors.

CHAPTER TEN

Donavin, Spoon, and J.R. arrived back in Atlanta shortly before eight P.M. Their three-bedroom apartment in the upscale Buckhead section of Atlanta was just as they left it in May. They quickly unloaded their belongings and chilled for the remainder of the evening. Exhausted, the men sat at their kitchen table and began to discuss the year to come.

"Brothers," Spoon began, "this being the final year of our collegiate careers, the Billion Dollar Playboys must do things bigger and better than ever before. I'm talking about women, limousines, champagne, and caviar."

"Ain't no doubt, dawg!" J.R. answered. "We need to put a hurtin' on deez breezies. I'm gittin' so many girls dis year. History is gon' speak 'bout me and Wilt Chamberlain in da same sentence!"

"I wholeheartedly agree," Donavin responded with confidence. "This is our year. No half-steppin'."

"What is you talking 'bout, dawg. You in love wit' Jasmine. I saw da look on yo' face when we lef' dis mornin'. You ain't foolin' nobody."

"Whateva, Big Country. You just make sure that you get plenty of rest so you can keep up with me."

Spoon looked directly into each of his friends' eyes. "Tomorrow, it's on."

That night Donavin lay in bed with his thoughts again on Jasmine. He knew his friends wanted him to act wild and enjoy his senior year with reckless abandon, but he felt a respect for her, an understanding. He didn't want to jeopardize the trust that she'd placed in him, but she understood his situation and wasn't pressing him to be in a relationship. After all, he was a Billion Dollar Playboy.

New student orientation at Stratford was a time for freshman to get adjusted and upperclassmen to come back early for a week of easy living, scoping out the new prospects, and partying. Thursday was a little late to come back, but the BDP never did things in a conventional way.

They got up early the next morning and headed to campus in J.R.'s ride. Their first stop was the Student Government Association office in Rogers Hall. The guys had Stratford on lock this year; Donavin was SGA president, Spoon was the vice president, and J.R. was the treasurer.

They made calls and set up back-to-school events in order to let everyone know that they were back in town. At Stratford, the SGA's only real responsibility was to set up tight parties. After a morning of hard work and two parties planned, they figured it was time to strut their BDP stuff on the Quad.

It was a beautiful, cloudless day of about eighty-five degrees. They sauntered to the Quad and approached a sea of students who were busy posting up—standing around in the latest fashions, socializing and posturing. At this, the BDP were masters. They all wore tank tops to show off their muscles with fresh new shorts, kicks, and sunglasses. It was the custom to have music on the Quad on nice days. The DJ was playing the R. Kelly and Jay-Z remix of

"Fiesta" as they came onto the scene, and all attention turned indubitably to them. They felt the stares of many anxious young ladies and enjoyed every second of it.

"Hey, Donavin, looking good," greeted Angela Troublefield, staring at Donavin like she was a woman in the desert and he was a tall drink of water.

Angela was a fair-skinned woman with voluptuous breasts, a tiny waist, and beautifully groomed brown hair with light brown streaks. Her legs were long and smooth, and she had a behind that could make a grown man cry. On a scale of one to ten she was a twelve. Angela was the chapter president of Epsilon Sigma Chi, the elitist sorority on campus, as well as a Hawks cheerleader.

"Hey yourself, Angela. Why don't you come here and give me a hug?"

She embraced him tightly.

"So Ange, are you going out for Miss Stratford this year?"

"Yes, I am. You're coordinating the event, right?"

"It's one of my duties as president."

"What are your other duties?" Angela gently stroked his chest with her right hand.

"Give me your number and we'll discuss it later."

Angela scribbled down her number on a piece of paper from her leather Franklin planner and handed it to him. She kissed him on his cheek and went on her way. Donavin felt good about how she had just so blatantly hit on him.

J.R. looked over his sunglasses. "Ooh wee! Double Troublefield! Dawg, her titties is so big! I sure hope you smash dat up in da near future!"

Donavin smiled and said, "I'm not pressed. That'll be there whenever I want it."

They walked on past a host of their friends and female acquaintances and caught up on everyone's summer activities. The BDP relished telling everyone how they conquered New York.

Spoon saw him first. "Don't look now, gentlemen, but here comes Little Dicky."

Donavin and J.R. turned to see their archenemy, Richard Smithers, strutting their way. He was a member of the fraternity Beta Alpha Delta, and the BDP absolutely despised him and most of his frat brothers.

Smithers was about 5'5" tall with a mouth the size of Texas. He was one of those brothers who wore a suit to class every day even though he barely had a 2.0 GPA. Smithers ran against Donavin in the SGA race and was defeated by a margin of ten to one—those "ones" being his frat brothers. That was yet another reason for their animosity toward each other.

"Donavin! How are ya, buddy?" Smithers greeted Donavin in a tone as fake as he was.

Donavin looked over the rim of his sunglasses, shook his head, and started to walk off. He thought very little of Smithers and cared even less for his false demeanor.

"Don't ever turn your back on me!" Smithers grabbed Donavin's arm.

The tension was felt by everyone on the Quad, and a circle formed around them almost immediately, including some of Smithers' frat brothers. Smithers was too much of a coward to face him alone, so he thought that creating a scene in front of a large group of people might give him some juice.

Donavin yanked his bicep from Smithers' grasp and turned around. He looked at the diminutive Smithers and said, "Negro, if you ever put your hands on me again, it'll take all of your Beta girl-friends to remove my foot from your ass."

Spoon and J.R. backed Donavin and stood firm. They were ready for an all-out brawl. Now there were about six Betas behind Smithers. It was three on seven, but the BDP was confident. Most

Betas didn't exactly look like linebackers. They had each Beta by at least fifty pounds.

Just then an authoritative voice said, "Break it up! Move on, people! Move on!" Campus police quickly quelled the disturbance.

"This isn't over! Watch your back, Jackson!" Smithers yelled as his brothers restrained him.

"Shut your punk ass up!" the BDP yelled back in unison.

The dispersing crowd erupted in laughter and Smithers felt embarrassment at being publicly slighted by the BDP. Donavin, Spoon, and J.R. laughed and gave each other dap for another great performance.

"Man, I don't even know why we pay attention to that Mini-Me-lookin' fool," Donavin said, mocking Smithers further.

J.R shook his head. "Dawg, I so hope one of us gets to whoop his ass befo' we graduate."

"How does one's parents let them grow up to be such an ass-hole?" Spoon said dryly.

Donavin was now over it and had other thoughts on his mind. "So, what's up for tonight, my brothers?"

J.R. grinned because he had what he thought was a brilliant idea. "Peep dis. I say we go to da package sto', git some liquor, call some breezies, and have a welcome-back party."

"Wow!" Spoon exclaimed. "Something really is going on in that brain of yours. That's a capital idea. Let's get on it."

They mingled amidst the Quad crowd a bit more and told only the finest women they could find about their little soireé. People couldn't get the details fast enough because everyone knew that a BDP party was always the spot.

The afternoon passed rapidly after more posting up on the Quad, and they decided to head home to get their place ready for their guests. Donavin went home and gave Jasmine a call at work while Spoon and J.R. handled the task of liquor acquisition.

"Simon and Rothstein, Jasmine DeRoche speaking."

"Hello, Simon and Rothstein Jasmine DeRoche speaking."

"Donavin!" Jasmine smiled widely into the receiver.

"Hey, Baby Girl."

"Hey, Brown Eyes. Nice trip?"

"It was cool. I miss you already."

Jasmine paused, briefly taken aback. "Oh . . . I miss you, too. So, are the girls knocking down your door yet? How many numbers have you gotten so far?"

Donavin pulled Angela's number from his pocket and placed it on his desk.

"You ask a lot of questions!" Donavin joked, skillfully avoiding answering her.

"Sorry. So what's the plan for tonight?"

"A party at the BDP Penthouse. We were out promoting it a little earlier. It should be a nice turn-out."

"A party at the BDP Penthouse, huh? You guys live in a penthouse?"

"It's pretty nice, but it's not a penthouse per se. That's just our nickname for it."

"So where's my invite to the BDP Penthouse."

"You know you're welcome any time."

"How about you make a trip up here next weekend? My treat."

"Your treat? That's very generous of you. You're on. Hey, the fellas and I are running the show at Homecoming this year. How about you come down that weekend and be my date for the ball? My treat."

"That's a date as well. I won't hold you. Go get ready for your party. I'll talk to you later, Brown Eyes."

Donavin hung up the phone and got busy trying to find a DJ for the party. He dialed Winston Charles' number, and he picked up the first ring.

Winston was a computer science major and wannabe member of the BDP. A year behind them, he often made himself a nuisance as he wanted very much to be a part of their clique. But he was short, not particularly handsome, and definitely not the snappiest dresser in the world. The group kept him around because he ran errands for them and would pay cover charges and buy drinks whenever they went to clubs. He was also a very capable DJ and a genius when it came to anything related to computers.

"Winston, this is Donavin."

"Donavin! What's up, boy? How was your summer? You guys never called me from New York."

"Oh, my bad." Donavin smiled, trying not to sound sarcastic. "The summer was cool. Listen, we are in dire need of a DJ for a party we're throwing tonight at the BDP Penthouse. Can you help us out?"

"No problem. What time?"

So easy. Too easy. Donavin stifled a chuckle.

"Can you start setting up at about eight so you can be spinning by the time our guests arrive?"

"I'll be there at 7:59. This is awesome! See ya later, D!"

Shortly after ten, guests began to trickle in. Among the first to get there was Angela Troublefield with five of her Epsilon sisters looking very delicious in red and black sorority jackets and minidresses.

"Come on in, ladies." Donavin cordially welcomed them. "Have a drink and relax."

Angela replied, "We heard that the party at the BDP Penthouse was the place to be."

"You heard correct. You're looking fine as usual."

"Aren't you the charmer? I've got my eye on you." She turned and brushed his chin with her hand.

J.R. and Spoon were in the kitchen entertaining the ladies and encouraging them to consume as much alcohol as possible. From there, the party took on a life of its own. The female-to-male ratio was about four to one and the BDP was in its glory.

"Where the Party At" by Jagged Edge thumped through the speakers, the ladies were beautiful, and everyone enjoyed the festivities. The middle of the living room looked like a nightclub, especially when the BDP started a Soul Train line.

First, J.R. came through the line doing a dance that resembled smacking a girl on the behind. Then it was Spoon's turn. He came through doing a dance that looked like he was brushing lint off his shoulders because he was just so fresh and so clean. Donavin did the snake from one side of the line to the other, dancing with every cute girl that he saw.

After a while, Donavin grew tired of dancing and decided to take a break. He slipped away to his room to relax for a few minutes before rejoining the party and plopped down onto his bed.

Angela watched Donavin retire to the back of the apartment and followed him. She stood outside his door for a few minutes and slipped in when she thought no one was looking. Donavin sat up immediately.

"Whew! It's hot out there. I thought I'd take a little breather in here with you." Angela walked in fanning herself, then closed the door behind her.

Donavin replied, "Is that right?" He knew what she was there for and was not comfortable with the situation. He liked to be discreet about his business and only told Spoon and J.R. about his exploits. With so many people at the party, there was bound to be speculation.

"You look like you could use a massage." Angela sat next to him on the bed and began to rub his shoulders. "Ooh, you're so tense."

"That sounds good, and feels even better, but I don't want to be rude to my guests. Perhaps another time." Donavin slowly got up and opened the door.

"Are you sure? I've never had any complaints about my massages."

"My guests," he said politely, but firmly. "I really must get back. Thanks, though."

He headed out of the room and thought nothing of the encounter because nothing happened. However, everyone saw them leave his bedroom together. He may as well have announced it on the front page of the *Stratford Observer*.

The telephone rang itself into Donavin's dream. It wasn't until the third ring that he realized the phone was actually ringing. He clamored to answer before his machine picked up.

"Hello," he said groggily.

"How was the party, Brown Eyes?"

"Huh? Brown party?"

Jasmine laughed. "Sounds like someone partied a little too much."

"What time is it?" Donavin asked, finally regaining his senses.

"It's ten o'clock. What time did the party end?"

Donavin yawned and stretched. "Ah man, we didn't wrap up until about five."

"Five, huh? Well, excuse me."

"Yeah, it was a little out of control. It was definitely a groove."

"Good to hear." Jasmine smiled.

"Oh, Donavin," a woman's voice suddenly called from the living room. "Come here, honey."

What in the hell? Who in the hell?

"Um . . . hold on a second, Jas," he said, hoping that she didn't hear what he heard. He covered the receiver and peeked into the living room to see who it was.

Angela Troublefield lay stretched out on the leather couch.

"Ange, just be quiet, and I'll deal with you in a second," he whispered.

He ducked back into his room and removed his hand from the receiver.

"Hey, sorry about that. It seems we have a straggler from last night."

"Is that right?" Jasmine's attitude burned through the phone wires. "Funny how your only straggler seems to be of the female persuasion, wouldn't you say? And why is she calling you 'honey'?"

"Whoa! Hold up right there," he defended himself. "I didn't even know she was here. I promise you. I was just in my room chillin'. Alone."

"Whatever, Donavin. You have nothing to prove to me. I have no expectations of you anyway." Venom dripped from Jasmine's voice.

"No, I really didn't do anything. I'm like actually innocent for once."

"Innocent, huh? Look Donavin, that's your business. Work it out. I gotta go. I'll talk to you later." She hung up the phone abruptly.

Donavin threw the cordless phone on the bed and stormed into the living room. "Ange, what the fuck are you doing here?"

"Don't get mad, Donavin. I wanted to stay and make you breakfast when you woke up. You know, to thank you for throwing such a tight party."

Donavin thought about her proposition for a second. He was mad as hell, but he was hungry, too. "Fine. Do your thing then."

"Well, I'd like to get a shower before I start cooking. Is that okay?"

"The bathroom is down the hall."

"I thought I saw a private bathroom in your room last night? I wouldn't want Spoon or J.R. to walk in on me."

"My towels are in my bathroom closet," Donavin said reluctantly.

"Thanks. Why don't you come in and join me? I hate to waste water."

"I'm straight. Maybe another time."

"I'll be out in a couple. Don't go anywhere." Angela winked at Donavin, then disappeared into his room.

Donavin flopped down on the couch and J.R. and Spoon both came dragging themselves into the living room minutes later.

J.R looked at Donavin strangely. "Hey, dawg. Whose voice was dat? You git some ass last night? Dat's so positive!"

"The voice you heard was Angela's, but I didn't hit it. I didn't even know her ass—"

"And what a fine ass it is," Spoon interrupted. Donavin shot him a mean look. "But I digress. Please continue."

"So, there I am sleeping and I get a wake-up call from Jasmine. We're talkin' and then the next thing I know Angela opens her big mouth. To make a long story short, Jasmine hears, goes off on me, and hangs up the phone with hella attitude."

Spoon was intrigued. "An attitude, you don't say? What's the deal with you two? You hit it, didn't you? Yes! You completed the trifecta. I had faith in you the whole time. So how was it, my good man?"

J.R.'s jaw dropped. "How dare you say nuttin' dis whole time, dawg?"

"Anyway, I'm kinda feeling Jas. I'm supposed to see her in New York next week."

"So what's da problem? I say you hit Angela down here and you beat Jasmine up dere. I know you ain't tryna settle down and raise no nappy headed kids anytime soon. Hittin' da both of 'em makes perfec' sense to me," J.R. reasoned.

"I say the same, D. Angela is fine, willing, and probably very able. Do yourself a favor."

"Jasmine's a good girl. I'm not trying to screw her over like that."

"Ol' sof' ass Negro. I neva thought I'd see da day I would hear Donavin Jackson sound like a li'l bitch. You betta git Angela to make you some Bitch Flakes for breakfast 'cause you soundin' mighty ho-like."

"Fuck you, you country bastard. I ain't no bitch."

"Now, now boys," Spoon said, trying to calm tempers. "D, you have to do whatever is right for you. We're merely saying that if a girl like Angela wants it, then give it to her good like a Billion Dollar Playboy would." J.R. gave Spoon a pound in agreement.

"I know, I know," said Donavin, calming down. "My bad, J.R. This shit is just getting to me. I don't think I'm gonna go down that Angela road, though. Too much drama. She'll go around telling everybody and their mother. I kinda want to see where this Jasmine thing goes."

"You're so sweet." Spoon pinched Donavin's cheek.

"Whateva. I'll just smooth things over with Jasmine later. No reason not to get breakfast served to me now, though."

"Hold up. Dat broad spent da night jus' to cook yo' punk ass some breakfast fuh real? Man, send her to my room. I'll beat it up a few times for you."

"Donavin, can you come here a second?" Angela called from his bedroom.

"Your woman's calling you." Spoon joked.

J.R. and Spoon knew it was time to let Donavin operate and they both went back into their rooms.

Donavin walked into his bedroom. "Ange, what's up?" He was greeted with the sight of Angela lying across his bed with a towel covering her behind.

"Oh, nothing, honey. I was just wondering if you could rub some lotion on my back," Angela said, holding up Donavin's bottle of Lubriderm.

"Lotion?"

"Yeah, you are familiar, aren't you? It moisturizes the skin."

They both laughed and Donavin sat next to her on the bed. He took the lotion into his hands and began to rub her shoulders. Her skin smelled clean and it was so soft to his touch.

"How are you gonna get the rest of my back with this towel on?"

Now Donavin's interest was piqued. Angela's body was truly something to behold, and she looked sexy as hell lying there wearing nothing but the towel.

"I don't know," he replied. "Looks like we just have to work around it."

Without warning, she threw off the towel and lay there nude.

"Ange . . ." Donavin was now seriously fighting himself, but he averted his eyes nonetheless. She was ready and he knew it. He was aroused, but he knew he shouldn't because it would simply bring on more problems than he cared to deal with.

"Yes, Donavin," she said. His name sounded hypnotic as it rolled off her tongue.

"Ange, I sure am hungry. How about that breakfast, girl?"

"You haven't done anything to work up an appetite." She rolled over to expose herself fully.

Donavin jumped up from the bed and started to put on his sneakers. "You know, Mickey D's is right up the block."

Angela chuckled. "Okay, okay, fine. I can take a hint. Let me get dressed and hook up a little something for you."

"Cool. I'll let you have some privacy." Donavin practically ran out of his room and closed the door.

Angela put her clothes on and made her way to the kitchen where Donavin waited. She opened all of the cabinets and the aroma of bacon, French toast, and eggs began to fill the room shortly afterward. They sat together and began to eat.

"You're a good cook, Ange."

"Thanks. I hope you'll let me cook for you again really soon."

Donavin barely paid her any attention because he was stuffing his face.

"So, how are plans going for Miss Stratford?"

"This year's production is going to be hot, unlike last year when the Betas ran it. What a disaster. I was embarrassed for them. You looking forward to running?"

Angela replied with conviction, "I'm looking forward to winning. You can keep the first and second runner-up slots."

Donavin raised an eyebrow as he poured more syrup on his French toast. "Ambition. I like. We're gonna start selecting the girls for the pageant next week. You'll see the sign-up sheets. But be sure you holla at me." He glanced at her eyes momentarily and then continued to eat.

"I definitely will."

After eating and shooting the breeze a while longer about being seniors, Angela prepared to leave.

"Thanks for the breakfast, Ange. That was *really* nice of you."

"Thanks for the shower and the lotion. That was *really* nice of you." She reached up to give him a hug and he obliged. They embraced for a moment and then she seductively kissed him on the neck until she felt him begin to pull away. Angela released him from her grasp and strutted to her car.

Donavin stood in the doorway and watched her drive away, rubbing his neck where her lips had rested.

CHAPTER
ELEVEN

Jasmine and Stacia met at the lounge and restaurant SOL on the corner of Clermont and Dekalb in Brooklyn. They sat at the bar and ordered jumbo shrimp.

"Jas, you heard about the party the boys had last night?"

"I surely did," answered Jasmine with an attitude.

"One of my sorors spent the night over there, from what I understand."

"I called Donavin this morning and I heard some girl in the background. Who was it?"

"Angela Troublefield."

"Oh, really?"

Stacia could hardly wait to spill the beans. "Yeah, I heard that he was rubbing her down with lotion and telling her how much he liked her, among other things. He even said that he would take a shower with her. I mean, damn. He's been there for two days, Jas."

"And you fucked his boy on the first date," Jasmine said coldly. Her head and heart began to pound, and a mixture of jealousy and embarrassment came over her.

"Look, I'm fine with what happened between me and Adam. I'm just trying to let you know so you don't carry a flame for this

Donavin character."

"Thank you," Jasmine snapped.

"Let's change the subject. I see you're getting a little upset."

"I'm tired. It's been a long day. I'm going to leave you my part of the bill."

Jasmine shoved the money onto the bar and exited. She was extremely pissed. She hated the fact that Stacia already knew everything that had gone on despite her living in New York. Jasmine usually prided herself on making well thought-out decisions so she didn't want to judge Donavin without hearing his side, but things didn't sound at all positive to her.

Donavin decided to give Jasmine a few days to cool down. He didn't know what she was thinking, but he knew that she was mad for what happened Friday morning. Monday was the first day of class and he decided that he would try to call and make peace between Corporate Finance and Money and Banking.

"Simon and Rothstein, Jasmine DeRoche speaking."

"Jasmine, don't say anything, just listen. Look, I know what you thought you heard, but it's not like that. It's a big misunderstanding."

"You have absolutely nothing to explain to me." The tone in her voice cold and dry.

"Humor me. Angela stayed over, but I didn't even know. Nobody did."

"So then you decided that since she was there, why not rub lotion all over her little stank ass. Why not, Donavin? I mean since she was there and all."

"Huh? What!" he stammered. "Who told you that?"

Jasmine exhaled loudly into the receiver. "Is that really important?"

"Yes, because it's bullshit. People are haters, Jas. I'm doing my thing and people always have shit to say about that. I'll admit it. She did make me breakfast, but then she left. That was it." He left out the part about the lotion, feeling that she really didn't need to hear the specifics.

"Donavin, all I'm saying is be a better playa than that. If you're gonna be Mr. Billion Dollar Playboy, at least be discreet about it."

Annoyed at the flip comment Donavin responded, "Look, I'm chillin'. Nothing happened. Okay?"

"If you say so. I still want you to come this weekend. I mean I already got your ticket so you might as well. Your flight is for three on Friday."

"Thank you, Jas. And you know I still want to come this weekend, too. Look, we both know how rumors get started, and you know how it is here. Everyone is always talking about everyone else's business. If you want anything to work out between us, then you have to listen to me and not what other people say."

"Okay, but please don't mistake my trust for stupidity. Understand?"

"Understood."

"I gotta go, but please give Miss Troublefield my regards."

Jasmine hung up the phone. Her trust in him was shaken, but not gone at her first taste of what it was like to be in Donavin's world.

CHAPTER TWELVE

Donavin arrived at La Guardia Airport at a quarter to six and caught a cab to Jasmine's apartment. During the entire ride, he was worried about how she would receive him.

"Hello, Donavin." She peered out from behind the door with the chain lock still on.

"Hey, Baby Girl. Can I come in?"

Jasmine looked him up and down and nonchalantly replied, "I don't know. Can you?"

"Don't tell me you're still mad at me."

Jasmine shut the door but did not release the locks.

Ain't this about a bitch. I came all this way for her to act silly? Screw it. I'm going to my momma's.

He made an about-face and walked down the hallway, refusing to be drawn into what he deemed a childish game. Right before he was about to walk down the stairs he heard her voice.

"Oh, Donavin . . ."

He looked back, but he could not see her face. All he could see was her long caramel leg wrapped around the door.

"Leaving so soon?"

Donavin smiled, relieved that things were cool—at least for the time being. He walked back toward her and noticed that all she wore was a red silk robe. "So, what'cha got under that robe?"

"Oh . . . nothing," she said, releasing the belt at her waist and exposing her flesh.

Jasmine pulled Donavin into the apartment by his shirt. She started to lead him to the bedroom, but he stopped her. Donavin cleared the mail and the newspapers that were on her dining table with one swipe of his hand, and lifted Jasmine onto the table. Donavin parted her robe and stared at her body. He raised one of her legs in the air and began kissing her pedicured feet. His lips traveled down her leg until he made his way to her center. He began to tease her clitoris with long strokes of his tongue. Her body shuddered as Donavin increased the intensity. She shifted her hips and her moans grew louder. Jasmine shivered as she exploded into orgasmic bliss. She panted heavily, sweat glistening on her body.

Donavin stood to undress. He grabbed a condom from his nearby backpack and rolled it on. Then he flipped Jasmine onto her stomach and began to give her long powerful strokes.

"Harder!" she demanded.

He obliged and Jasmine matched each stroke with a pelvic thrust of her own. They moved faster and faster until Jasmine screamed and Donavin grunted. Their bodies tensed as they came together. Exhausted from their session, they lay almost lifeless, bodies soaked with sweat.

"You're gonna have to carry me to the bed, Brown Eyes. I can't move."

"You think I can?"

He lifted her into his arms, then carried her to the bedroom. They fell asleep in each other's carress.

Jasmine's cell phone had been ringing practically the entire time he'd been there, but since Donavin had his hands full from the get-go he'd ignored it. Now it was waking him up every ten minutes.

Jasmine, too, was awakened, but she pretended to be asleep. She hoped that the incessant ringing would stop. After it went off three more times within five minutes, she got up and turned it off.

"Who's trying to get in touch with you so crucially?"

"Nobody," she replied, getting back into bed and snuggling closer.

Donavin hardly believed that "nobody" was calling her, but he didn't press the issue.

Around four in the morning, several forceful knocks on the door awakened Jasmine. It sounded like the police or some other law enforcement authority. Jasmine sprang out of bed, grabbed her robe and practically ran to the door before the person knocked again and woke Donavin. But it was too late. Donavin was already awake. He heard Jasmine unlocking the door, then her hushed voice.

"I can't believe you. What are you doing here?" Jasmine spat.

"I followed one of your neighbors in. What's wrong with you?" a man's voice returned. "I'm calling you all this time and you don't pick up or call me back. You got somebody over here?"

"That's not your business. You need to leave. I'll talk to you later." Jasmine attempted to close the door.

"This is bullshit, Jasmine. Where is that muthafucka?" He stuck his foot in and pushed against the door with all his weight.

The two began to wrestle for control of the doorway and the sound of struggling impelled Donavin from the bed. He wanted to make sure that Jasmine was all right.

Son of a bitch! Donavin headed toward the door leading to the living room. *She was giving me all this drama and she's got a little somethin' on the side.*

He caught sight of the man trying to gain entry into the apartment.

I'll be damned!

It was Allen Pearson, Stratford graduate and former chapter president of the Betas.

Donavin gritted his teeth and clenched his fists. He became filled with rage. His first inclination was to interfere and kick Allen's ass, then his better judgement took over and he decided to go back to bed and act as if he hadn't seen a thing. Donavin slid back under the covers and closed his eyes.

If Miss Jasmine wants to play games, games I'll give her.

Jasmine finally won the battle of the doorway after fifteen minutes of arguing, pushing, and pulling, and rejoined Donavin in the bedroom as if nothing had happened.

Donavin awoke to light kisses on his face. He was thinking that if she were honest about what happened the night before, he would not resort to treating her like other women. However, they had breakfast, lunch, and dinner without her saying a word about the incident. They got along just fine, but Donavin was disappointed that she didn't choose to offer some kind of explanation.

After dinner, they decided to go to a late movie at the Court Street Theater to catch *Rush Hour 2*. They entered the theater and sat down with their popcorn and sodas.

Jasmine wrapped her arm around Donavin's and snuggled into his shoulder. "I'm so happy you're here, Brown Eyes. Aren't you?"

"Yeah, downright ecstatic."

Jasmine didn't pick up on his sarcasm and kissed him on the cheek. Donavin stuffed a handful of popcorn into his mouth.

"Let me use the restroom before the movie starts. I'll be right back."

"Cool. I'll be here."

Jasmine rose and turned to walk down the row. She'd only gone a few seats when she caught sight of Allen sitting a few rows back.

Jasmine spun on her heels and ran back to her seat. She shrank into the chair.

Donavin was surprised by her sudden return. "Um . . . that was quick."

"You know, I remembered that the bathrooms here are nasty. I'll just hold it."

Donavin eyed her strangely. "What's wrong?"

"Nothing," she replied, cowering in her seat and holding a hand across her brow.

"Oh, really?" He turned around and quickly scanned the crowd until he saw what she had. Allen and Donavin locked eyes and glared at each other. Donavin shook his head in disbelief. "Excuse me, Jasmine," he said, standing.

"Where are you going?" she asked frantically.

"Just to say hello to an old friend of mine. I'll be right back."

She grabbed his arm in protest.

"Relax, Jas. I won't be long." He strolled casually toward Allen.

"Allen." Donavin greeted him with a blank expression.

"Donavin. Beautiful lady you're with. It's a shame she doesn't keep better company."

Donavin leaned toward Allen. "It's kind of funny how we're here together and you have nothing better to do than follow us around. You're a pathetic little bastard."

Allen moved as if to stand and defend himself, but Donavin pushed him back in his seat with one finger.

"Allen, I thought you learned in school that I'm not the one to be fucked with. I'm sure you remember the ass kickin' you received the last time." Donavin laughed and said, "See ya 'round."

Donavin walked away as casually as he'd approached and returned to his seat beside Jasmine while Allen sat there seething. Mortified, Jasmine stared straight ahead, doing her best to look cool.

"Did you say hello to your friend?" Jasmine asked, as if she had no idea what was going on.

"Yeah, something like that."

The lights in the theater dimmed and the previews began. The tension between the two was palpable. Jasmine was not sure how to deal with Donavin's calm and collected manner. She wondered what he knew and what she should have told him.

The movie ended and Donavin quickly moved toward the exit, leaving Jasmine several steps behind. Apparently, Chris Tucker's antics weren't quite enough to cool him out. She rushed to catch up with him because she feared that he might be looking to pick a fight with Allen. Unbeknownst to her, her Beta buddy slipped out long before the credits began to roll.

"Is something wrong, Brown Eyes?" Jasmine asked as they walked out of the theater and down the street.

"Nope. Why would something be wrong?"

Jasmine pushed for an answer. "Yes, there is. Talk to me."

"I'm cool. Just tired is all." He shrugged her off.

"You seem like you're tired of me."

Stoically Donavin replied, "Don't push it, Jasmine. Respect what I said."

Jasmine slowed down and braced herself for what she was about to say. "Is this about Allen Pearson?"

Donavin stopped walking at the mention of his name. "I don't know, Jasmine. Is it? Do you have something to tell me about him? Like why he's at your door at four in the fucking morning?"

Jasmine's eyes widened. "Oh, you saw?"

"'Oh, you saw?' Do I look stupid? You thought you could make all that noise and I wouldn't go see what was going on? I was asleep, not in a fucking coma!"

"I'm sorry for what happened, but he likes me. We dated a few times in the summer, but that was before I started seeing you. I think he feels like I'm dissin' him because I've been choosing to spend time with you."

"Jas, me and that kid are like mortal enemies. It's come to blows before. Of all the people."

"He's really a nice guy."

"He's an elitist asshole just like the rest of the Betas."

"Look at you, Mr. High and Mighty. If I recall, you had an overnight sorority guest last week."

"That was different. We had a party and she stayed behind. None of us knew that she was there."

"Well, I believe you. Try believing me."

Donavin was not big on believing the word of females, but he decided to make an exception. He saw no point in pursuing the argument any further. As they faced one another, challenging each other with their eyes, Jasmine suddenly threw her arms around his neck and kissed him beneath the streetlight.

For the rest of the night, they enjoyed each other's company to the fullest; the fact that they didn't have much time left before he went back to school was ever present in their minds. When they arrived home, they alternated between making love and taking naps until he had to leave for the airport in the morning.

Jasmine accompanied Donavin to his gate and sat with him. "Thank you for your visit, Brown Eyes. I enjoyed you even when you were being an ass to me."

"Whatever. You just keep dudes out of your apartment at four in the morning—or four in the afternoon for that matter." He chuckled and kissed her on the forehead. "Next time, my place?"

"You got it."

His flight was called for boarding and each knew that it was time to say their goodbyes.

"Aight, Baby Girl. Looks like this is me."

"Sure is."

"I'll miss you."

"Me too." Jasmine drew close to him, burying her face in his chest. He kissed her one last time and disappeared all too quickly down the ramp.

Spoon and J.R. held up a sign that read "Billion Dollar Playboy Donavin Jackson," which Donavin immediately spotted upon entering the terminal at Hartsfield International Airport. Donavin smiled broadly at his friends' ingenuity.

"The sign was J.R.'s idea," Spoon said as he gave Donavin dap.

"Dat's right, dawg. Deez breezies know dey betta recognize."

"You brothers are wild."

"How was the weekend, sir?" Spoon asked.

"Let's ride out. I'll speak on it in the car."

The three men got in J.R.'s Navigator, or the Country Cruiser as they called it, and Donavin began his story.

"Fellas, remember that walking piece of shit Allen Pearson?"

J.R. was instantly riled at the mere mention of the name. "Man, I hope you neva defile da Country Cruiser by utterin' dat fool's name up in here one mo' gen."

"Ah, your former nemesis. What did you two kids get into it about again?"

Donavin refreshed their memories. "Remember Spirit Night during freshman orientation?"

J.R. looked confused as Spoon nodded and said, "I remember it well. Proceed."

"All the freshman dudes were parading around the campus, each man's hands on the man's shoulders in front of him. You know, the whole black male solidarity deal. I was on the lookout because I had heard stories of upperclassman trying to haze cats in the line. I must not have been paying that much attention because that fool slapped me in the back of my head. You know I immediately broke ranks and tackled his bitch ass. Then I made him kiss the ground. I made him like actually open his mouth and lick that shit with his tongue. I had to let him know that I wasn't the one."

"I remember dat shit. I was in line a few spaces behind you, dawg. You ain't lyin'. You did make dat fool French kiss da ground like a li'l bitch."

"Anyway, turns out that sorry muthafucka is in New York and he seems to have feelings for Jasmine. He comes knocking at her door late as hell Friday night. I wake up and I see them arguing at the door. I was about to run up and do a Rambo, but I just chilled in the cut. The next day she played it off and didn't even find it necessary to explain the situation to me. So we're at the movies, I look back and his ass had followed us to the damn show!"

"And you whooped his ass proper all up and down da theater, right?" J.R. asked as if it were a foregone conclusion.

"Nah, lock-up is a bitch. I wanted to, but it just wasn't worth my time."

"Well," Spoon began dryly, "be mindful. These ladies will certainly attempt to try a young brother. As is always the case with females, there's always plenty more going on behind the scenes that they don't tell you. Think about it. If you weren't getting any would you feel free to come a-knockin' in the middle of the night? I think not."

"True that, Spoon." Donavin agreed. "I don't trust her for shit. I'm just gonna do my thing. BDP through and through."

"BDP through and through," Spoon and J.R. said in unison.

CHAPTER THIRTEEN

It was a beautiful September morning in the city of Atlanta. Summer was ending and fall was fast approaching. The temperature was a perfect seventy-five degrees and humidity was null. The members of the BDP decided to go for a light jog and enjoy the morning.

"It's such a nice day out, bruthas. Today is gon' be bangin' on da Quad. Broads ain't gon' be wearin' no clothes," J.R. said, panting the last sentence through short breaths.

"I know, but Donavin is whipped on a Beta lover. I never thought I'd see the day." Spoon grinned.

"I don't know what you're talking about," Donavin replied. "Last weekend cured me of all of that. I'm gonna do my thing. I'm a playa. I'm movin' up to Trillion Dollar Playboy status this year. Watch me."

"Den when you gon' wax Angela's ass?" J.R. challenged.

Donavin frowned. "I'm not even concerned about that. Why am I gonna stress over some ass that's available to me twenty-four seven? Why don't you hit it for me, Big Country, and tell me how it is?"

"Don't play wit' me, boy. I'll tear dat ass up in new ways. Her weave'll be all fucked up and da broad won't walk straight no mo'."

"Fellas, I've had enough exercise." Spoon patted his brow. "I'm too pretty to be sweating like this outside the bedroom."

The others agreed and the three decided to head back to the apartment. Once at home they went straight to the kitchen for water.

"Dat was a good ass run. I might have to skip my classes and enjoy dis nice day," J.R. said. He never needed much of a reason to skip class. "What can go wrong on a day like dis?"

"You said something there, partner. I gotta drain myself. I'll be back." Donavin went to the bathroom.

"Yo Spoon, flip on dat Jerry Springer fuh a brutha," J.R. yelled from the kitchen where he was making toast.

Spoon eased onto the couch and pressed the power button on the remote control. He started flipping channels, but it was as if every channel was showing the same show.

"What the . . .?" It suddenly dawned on Spoon that what he saw was no television show but a real-life drama unfolding in real-time.

"Bruh, I said flip dat Springer on," J.R. said, mildly annoyed as he dropped onto the couch. He looked at the screen. "Oh shit! Is dat da World Trade Center?"

Spoon's glass shattered against the hardwood floor as he stared at the television screen. J.R. didn't notice as his attention was riveted to the news report as well. The scenes of carnage and mayhem were surreal to them, as if they were dreaming and would somehow wake up to find it wasn't true.

Donavin came back from the bathroom and noticed the grave looks on his friends' faces. He gazed at them with a puzzled expression. "What's with the long faces? No Jerry Springer today?"

Spoon and J.R. didn't answer—couldn't answer. They just sat blinking at the images on the screen. Donavin looked to see what held his friends speechless for once and then he, too, stared in disbelief with his mouth agape. He couldn't speak. He could barely breathe. Donavin immediately thought of Jasmine who worked in the World Financial Center, directly beside the Twin Towers.

Without uttering another word, he rushed to the phone in his room and frantically dialed her work number. He grew increasingly frustrated each time he received a busy signal. He tried her home and cell phone numbers with the same result. The fear that something had happened to her nearly paralyzed him. He knew that New York City was in a state of chaos, and he felt helpless because he was not there to protect her.

After pacing for a few minutes he noticed that the message light on his phone was blinking. He quickly pressed play to listen to the message.

"Donavin!" Jasmine cried, panic and terror cracking her voice. *"A plane just crashed into one of the World Trade Center towers! Everybody's freaking out! I'm so scared! Oh my God! Oh my God! There's another plane . . . no-o-o-o-o-o!"* She screamed. The message ended.

Donavin's whole body went numb. His breathing increased as if he were still jogging. With tears filling his eyes, the task of finding her consumed him. He ran to his closet, grabbed a suitcase in one hand and half a rack of clothes with the other. He filled the suitcase with as many clothes as would fit and rushed out of his room toward the front door.

"Where are you going?" Spoon asked, stepping in front of him and blocking his exit.

"New York. Jasmine works next door to the World Trade Center." Tears streamed down Donavin's cheeks. "She called me while the whole thing was going on. The phone went dead after the second plane hit."

J.R. put his hand on Donavin's shoulder. "Bruh, I know you want to find her, but New York is straight up crazy right now. Let's jus' pray dat da girls are okay."

"That's a good idea, J.R. Go get your Bible," Spoon said somberly and led Donavin to the kitchen table.

J.R. went to his room and got his leather bound Bible. He was a bit of a contradiction. He talked loudly, cursed, drank, and showed very little respect for women. However, he had a deep-seated spirituality and a belief in God that never faltered. He returned and they began to pray.

"Lawd," J.R. began, "Lawd, we pray for da souls of everyone we lost in dis attack on our country dis mornin'. We pray for yo daughtas, Jasmine, Stacia, and Carmen. Please keep dem safe and outta harm's way, Lawd. Please let us see dat da ugly way we treat each otha' jus' ain't right, Lawd. Give us da strength to overcome dis day, Lawd, and love one anotha' da way you meant fuh us to. Please let our friends live and continue to serve You on Earth, Lawd. In Jesus' name we pray. Amen."

"Amen," Spoon and Donavin repeated.

"Just keep trying her on her cell, D. I know she's okay. Just keep trying." Spoon encouraged, putting his arm around Donavin's shoulders. "I gotta check on my people in NY, too."

"Spoon, yo' family is in Long Island. Dat ain't New York already. Damn!"

Donavin kept trying to no avail. All three stayed home from class and watched the newscasts for the rest of the morning. Donavin felt badly for all the people who were hurt and lost their lives in the disaster, but he found solace in the fact that Jasmine's building was evacuated and still standing.

That afternoon he tried her cell phone again and finally it appeared to be going through. He waited with nervous anticipation as the phone rang.

"Hello," Jasmine whimpered.

"Oh my God! Jasmine, are you okay?"

"Brown Eyes! It's unbelievable here. There are millions of people in the streets all walking away from downtown. I've never seen this many people in the streets before. I can't believe this happened."

"Are you all right, Baby Girl?"

"Yeah." She sniffled and coughed. "I've just got a lot of dust on me."

"It's so good to hear your voice. When I got your message I was so shook that something might have happened to you."

"Shit, I was shook when I left it! All those poor people. I can't believe that somebody could do this. But I'm okay. I'm alive at least."

Donavin's other phone line clicked.

"Hold on a second, Jas."

He clicked over and it was his mother.

"Donny, are you kids okay? They blew up the World Trade Center. What is this world coming to?"

"Mom, we're all all right. Are you okay? Are you at school?"

"No, sweetie, I wasn't feeling well and I stayed home today."

"Thank God. Momma, I've got Jasmine on the other line. I'm on her cell phone. I'll call you right back."

"Oh! She's all right, isn't she?"

"Yeah, Mom, I'll call you right back." Donavin rushed her off the phone.

"I love you, Donny. Bye."

"Me too, Momma." He clicked back over. "I'm back, Baby Girl. Are Stacia and Carmen cool?"

"Yeah, they both work in Midtown. They're fine."

"Thank God. Look, I want you to go uptown to Stacia's in Harlem. I heard that they closed off the city."

"I'm on my way there now, Brown Eyes. Don't worry about me, but I gotta go now. I gotta save some battery to call my family. I miss you."

"I miss you, too." He hung up the phone and silently thanked God.

Donavin was filled with joy and relief at the fact that Jasmine was okay. The more he thought, the more he realized that he didn't know what he would have done if she hadn't been all right. Donavin cared about her regardless of what they were going through and he could not have handled it if she hadn't made it. Earlier that morning, he was talking about his ascension to a Trillion Dollar Playboy devoid of Jasmine. Not less than an hour later he was ready to get in his car and drive to New York to find her. Despite what he told his boys and what happened that weekend, his feelings for her continued to grow.

"Did you get through to Jasmine?" Spoon asked when Donavin rejoined them.

"Yeah," Donavin spoke, relief in his voice. "Stacia and Carmen are fine, too. Man, this is the wildest shit ever." He saw the images flash across the television screen once more and still found it hard to believe.

"We was jus' down dere drankin' like a few weeks ago, y'all." J.R. shook his head in disbelief. "How does somethin' like dis happen?"

Spoon looked down and said, "This is a wake-up call from hell. We definitely have to live each day to the fullest."

CHAPTER
FOURTEEN

Keyshawn Williams clapped his hands loudly, his silver bracelets jangling against each other in a wild rhythm.

"Places, people! Places!" Keyshawn sang out, his high-pitched voice carrying in the large auditorium. He stomped across the stage in platform snakeskin boots when the girls were slow to move. "We have a show to do, ladies. Thank you!"

Keyshawn took his job as director of the Miss Stratford Pageant very seriously, and he was determined to make this year's pageant a highly stylized and dramatic event.

"*Hel–lo*, am I talking to myself? This show is in three weeks. Let's get with it, ladies!" he ordered, snapping his fingers. Keyshawn continued to run the practice military style for the next two hours. If it had lasted any longer, he may have had a mutiny on his hands. He wasn't very tactful with the girls and didn't hesitate to tell many of them that they could stand to lose a few pounds.

After practice, Angela sashayed over to Donavin who was sitting with Spoon and J.R. joking about the way Keyshawn ran practice.

"Hey, D, you look sexy in your suit." Angela complimented him on his three-piece Ralph Lauren suit. As executive producer of the show he had to look the part.

"I'm not the sexy one. You seem to have that market cornered yourself," Donavin replied in kind, referring to Angela's black boots, black spandex pants, and black baby tee.

"You need to tell your boy, Keyshawn, that he's getting on everybody's nerves. Actin' like a little bitch. Walkin' around here talkin' 'bout 'you betta strut it betta than that, honey'. He is way too much."

"He's just trying to get y'all ready." Donavin tried to soothe her. "I'll ask him to turn it down a notch."

Angela smiled and raised her eyebrow. "We should hook up sometime when you get a chance."

"I'll be sure to take it under advisement."

Angela smiled again and went to rejoin the other pageant contestants who were leaving the auditorium.

"Man!" J.R. said. "If you don't hit dat, I will! Dat girl wants you so strong!"

"Don't you think I know that? Once again, I'm not pressed; she's not going anywhere," Donavin answered with an arrogant edge in his voice.

"I have to agree with J.R. on this one, D," Spoon added. Then a look of confusion came over his face. "You act like you're in love with Jasmine or something? Are you?"

"Nah, man, I'm just chillin' right now."

"Jus' chillin', huh?" J.R. looked at Donavin in disbelief. "Yo' happy ass wasn't jus' chillin' when you was 'bout to drive to New York."

"I was concerned is all. For real, I'm *just* chillin'."

Donavin wanted to convince his friends that he wasn't going soft by falling in love. He knew that his feelings for Jasmine were strong, but his friends didn't need to know it, too.

CHAPTER
FiFTEEN

Two days before the pageant everyone was busy finalizing last-minute details. For the past few weeks Donavin had spent a lot of time with Keysawn and the Miss Stratford contestants to make sure that the show would run smoothly—unlike the previous Beta-run fiasco.

Between school and the pageant, Donavin had little time for much else. He spoke with Jasmine sporadically over the last few weeks, though never for more than ten minutes at a time.

Although they were on decent terms, Jasmine became more and more distrustful of him. She heard through the Stacia grapevine that Angela had been spending a great deal of time with Donavin at pageant practices and she became increasingly jealous. She was scheduled to fly into Atlanta on Thursday night and she called Donavin to confirm her arrival.

"Donavin," she said benignly, "I was calling to see if you were still picking me up or if I should take a cab or get a rental."

"Huh?" He responded as if caught off guard. "Damn, girl, what's with all the hostility?"

"Just tell me what you're going to do so I can plan accordingly," Jasmine replied with even more attitude.

"Your flight lands at eight. I said that I'd get you and I will. What's the matter?" Donavin knew full well what the hostility was for, but he tried to play it off nonetheless.

"I'll see you tomorrow at the airport then." Jasmine hung up without another word.

Donavin shrugged his shoulders and put the phone in its cradle. He supposed that Jasmine had a right to be upset, but he was too tired to deal with it.

The final dress rehearsal for Friday's pageant was wrapping up. The ladies of Stratford were ready to put on a top-notch show. The BDP were making their final preparations, and even Keyshawn was satisfied with everything. The theme of the show was "Black to Africa," and the Egyptian-inspired set celebrated the beauty of the black woman from Africa to America.

Angela's costume was breathtaking. She wore an authentic Egyptian gown with a beautiful headdress. The outfit was revealing but very classy at the same time, and her beauty rivaled that of Queen Nefertiti. It was relatively certain that she would be this year's queen and that the first and second runner-up slots were the only ones up for debate.

Donavin stopped staring at Angela and casually looked down at his watch. "Oh shit," he muttered at the realization that the time was now 7:30.

"Fellas." Donavin turned to J.R. and Spoon. "I gotta go to the airport and scoop Jas up. I'll see you guys at home."

"Fine ass Jasmine? Hoodie hoo!" J.R. replied. "I know you mus' be itchin' to beat dat up. Keep it warm fuh me. I plan on layin' it down when I git home."

"No, my brotha. You gotta get your own," Donavin responded with quick wit.

Spoon pulled Donavin aside. "Donavin, there's a lot of talk going around about you and Angela. Everybody seems to be saying that you guys are on the verge of making it official. Her words, I'm sure. Just be mindful, D."

Donavin let out a sigh. "Damn, I figured that was why Jas was so pissed when I spoke to her yesterday. So many haters around here. Thanks for the info." He gave Spoon a pound and exited the auditorium.

Donavin went to the parking lot to get his car and came upon a roadblock. Angela had apparently skipped out of practice early because she was already waiting at his Mercedes. She had changed her clothes and was leaning against his car wearing tight black jeans and a black T-shirt that was tied in the front to expose her svelte abdomen.

"Skipping out a little early, I see," Angela drawled.

"Look who's talking," Donavin shot back. "I'm a busy man. I just have something I need to handle."

"Like what?" She drew closer to him as he moved toward his driver side door.

"Like stuff that little girls needn't concern themselves with."

"When you see a little girl, you let me know." Angela had a devilish look in her eye.

They were now inches from each other's face. Before he realized what was happening, Angela grabbed him aggressively by the shirt and kissed him on the lips. Against his better judgment, he kissed her back. After a few moments, Donavin pulled away.

"Ange, I really gotta go."

"Keep fighting. I like it rough."

Jasmine and Stacia flew in together on the same flight for the Homecoming festivities. As they descended into Atlanta, Stacia began heaping massive amounts of haterade on Donavin.

"Jas, my line sister told me that your boy, Donavin, has been getting awfully close to Angela Troublefield lately. She told me that they've been kickin' it hella hard."

"So what!" Jasmine snapped back.

"Touchy! I'm just trying to help you out."

"You know what, Stacia? As it pertains to Donavin, stay out of my business!"

"Whateva, Jas. Don't get mad when you get down there and things aren't the same." Stacia added fuel to the fire.

"Did I stutter, dammit? It's not any of your fucking business!"

Jasmine was livid. Donavin warned her what being in any kind of relationship with him was going to be like, but she didn't think it would be this hard. Jasmine thought that Angela's name was coming up too much for nothing to be going on.

After the plane touched down and the passengers disembarked, Jasmine picked up her bags and rushed off with Stacia scrambling to catch up. She ignored Stacia the entire trip to the baggage claim area. When she arrived at the luggage carousel Donavin greeted her with a dozen roses. Jasmine wanted to smile, but she was determined to stay mad at him.

"Hey, Baby Girl, I missed you." Donavin handed her the flowers and leaned in to kiss her. She turned her face and the kiss landed on her cheek.

"Hello, Donavin, how are you," Jasmine replied coldly. She took the flowers from his hands.

The tension was thick and Donavin thought that Jasmine must have an inkling as to what was going on. However, part of being a player was not to admit anything willingly. If she had an accusation to make, he was resigned to let her make it.

"What's the matter, Jas?" Donavin inquired.

"We'll talk in the car," Jasmine said through gritted teeth.

"Stacia's coming out behind me."

Stacia walked over to them and greeted Donavin with a pointed smirk. "Hey, Donavin."

"Stacia." Donavin answered her without a proper hello. He barely acknowledged her because he knew she was the one filling Jasmine's head with ugly rumors about him.

"Let's dip out, Donavin," Jasmine ordered. "I'll see you later, Stacia."

The silent walk to the car was as chilly as the Arctic itself. Donavin knew Jasmine was pissed off to the highest level of pisstivity.

"So Donavin," Jasmine said as he backed out of the parking space. "What have you been up to for the last few weeks? I've hardly even spoken to you." Her tone hinted that she was looking for Donavin to give himself up about Angela.

"I've just been busy planning Homecoming, going to school, et cetera, et cetera."

"Yeah, I'll bet," Jasmine answered sharply. "It's the 'et cetera' I'm worried about."

They had just merged onto Interstate 85 when Donavin suddenly swerved the car across four lanes of traffic. Jasmine gripped the door handle and closed her eyes until the car came to a screeching halt.

"Jasmine," Donavin said in a surprisingly calm tone, "if you have an issue with me, I suggest you make it known so we can talk about it and squash it. Quite frankly, I'm not going through whatever this is all weekend."

"I don't have an issue, Donavin. You can start driving again at any time," Jasmine answered in a tone that matched Donavin's.

After ten minutes of driving in icy silence, they arrived at the BDP Penthouse. Spoon and J.R.'s cars were outside and Donavin was happy that he was about to see some friendly faces.

Jasmine and Donavin entered the apartment and were greeted

by the sounds of Jill Scott on the stereo and the laughter of Spoon, J.R. and two of their female friends. The two girls were pageant contestants making a final push for the crown.

"Jasmine!" J.R. and Spoon greeted in unison.

"One o' deez days I'ma sop you up wit' a biscuit, girl," J.R. added.

Jasmine smiled for the first time since she got off the plane and gave both Spoon and J.R. hugs. Donavin could hardly believe that this was the same girl who'd been as frigid as an ice cube since he picked her up. He led her to the bedroom so she could put her things down.

As soon as they stepped into the room the phone rang. Donavin forgot to turn the ringer off before he left the house earlier. Turning the ringer off was in the player handbook just after never give yourself up. Donavin looked on the Caller ID and saw that it was Angela. Jasmine had already been trippin', so he thought he'd better come up with something. He decided to go ahead and answer.

"Hello," he spoke in a low tone.

"Hey, honey. I didn't think I'd get you. Your lips tasted so good earlier."

Donavin released an uneasy laugh. "Yeah? Oh, word? Aight den. Check it. Let me hit you back. Peace." He quickly hung up the phone before Angela could say anything else to make him blush.

This was just the ammunition Jasmine needed. She looked at him like he had just slapped her momma.

"Oh, I wish you hadn't hung up the phone without giving Miss Angela my regards. She's such a lovely girl!" Jasmine barked.

"Okay, so that's what this is all about? Look, I'm not even messing with her. We're just friends. Furthermore, I really don't see it being any of your business. You're not my girlfriend."

Donavin usually prided himself on thinking before he spoke,

but as soon as the words left his lips he wished he had left that last part off.

"Let me fucking tell you something!" Jasmine stuck her finger into Donavin's chest. "I am well aware of the fact that we are not together. Don't flatter your fucking self. Every woman in the world does not desire your sorry ass! You do whatever you want. You're not the only one with 'just friends'." She raised her hands to quote the air when she spat the words at him. "Don't worry about me because I'll do what I gotta do, just like you will."

"Come on, Jas," Donavin said, moving toward her as if to hold her. "This is nothing."

"No!" Jasmine pulled away. "Don't touch me! I don't know where you've been."

At this point, Donavin had taken the last insult he was going to take. All the guilt that he had felt for messing around with Angela earlier disappeared.

"All right now, this is bullshit," he said matter-of-factly. "At your age, you should really be woman enough not to act this way. I've got too much on my plate to deal with this nonsense this weekend."

"Don't then," Jasmine hissed. "I'm sure Miss Troublefield will be less *troublesome* for you."

"Jasmine," Donavin began, his voice calm and collected although he was irate, "I think you should stay with Stacia tonight. You're not going to disrespect me in my house. You should go cool out and I'll call you tomorrow."

"Wrong fucking answer!" Jasmine was defiant. "How about you don't call me and you find another date for your little bullshit ball. Fuck you!"

She wheeled her luggage out of the room and then out of the apartment. J.R. and Spoon giggled slightly as Jasmine exited and slammed the door. Donavin followed right behind her. "What the hell is so damned funny?" he snapped at his friends.

"Ol' angry ass fool," J.R. responded. "Need to go git yo' girl befo' a bruh like me pick it up on da rebound."

"What's going on?" asked Spoon. "That was a tad bizarre."

"That broad is acting like a lunatic is what's going on," he said to his boys before he realized that their company was still present. "Can you ladies excuse us? I have important business to discuss with these guys."

J.R.'s mouth dropped wide open speechlessly. He didn't want to openly contradict Donavin, but he was definitely upset as the ladies left.

"Hey, dawg, I was 'bout to beat so strong. What da hell couldn't wait 'til a post-beat discussion group?"

"That was rather rude, Mr. Jackson. You just performed the equivalent of snatching food off our plates."

"Both of you will live. I need to talk about the final preparations for the pageant tomorrow night. Everything as far as the tuxes and limo is already taken care of, however, there has been a change in the date structure. I decree that our dates should be the winner of the pageant and the two runners-up," said Donavin.

"Look at dis muthafucka. Jasmine heard 'bout you fuckin' 'round wit' Angela when y'all ain't even fuckin' and promptly gave you yo' walkin' papers. Ain't dis some shit. Now yo' ass tryna do damage control. Let me lay some knowledge on you as to why you ain't bein' successful right now. You ain't payin' attention in Corporate Finance."

"I know there's a spectacular explanation that goes along with this one." Spoon laughed.

"Git yo' pads and pencils 'cause I'm 'bout to school y'all fools. Most cute broads are like Internet stocks. Jus' highly overvalued relative to performance of da company. Dat's why a brotha like me gots to aggressively diversify his portfolio. What jus' happened was market risk bitin' you in da ass 'cause you only got one damn stock.

You got to hedge against dat by havin' multiple breezies. I can't believe dem fools at Proctor and Proctor gave you a full-time offer and you ain't applyin' basic financial principalities."

Spoon and Donavin burst into laughter as J.R. sat stone-faced.

"Dat was some ol' deep intellectual, philosophical shit. What y'all fools laughin' fuh?"

Donavin merely smiled. "Are you guys down for the date thing or what?"

"Don't you think it's a little late to announce this?" questioned Spoon.

"I hate to pull rank, but I *am* the President."

"So be it," Spoon acquiesced.

"Man, dem broads not only got a shot at da title, but dates wit' da BDP? Dey so damn lucky. Yo' ass lucky, too. You betta be glad me and Spoon didn't already have dates for da Ball. I neva did undastand why you invited Jasmine. Dat's like bringin' sand to da damn beach. Dere gon' be so many fine, single broads up in dat piece tomorrow. I suppose we can hook you up dis once, dough."

"Jasmine is going to kick your ass if she sees you with another chick the day after a fight, especially if you wind up escorting Angela. Are you sure you want the drama?"

"Spoon, I'm a playboy. A Billion Dollar Playboy at that. Taking another date to the ball is just a slight change in plans. I show up with another tight girl and that just raises my stock value. Jasmine will be angry initially and then want me more. I learned that in Playboy 101. I thought you knew?"

Spoon laughed. "I'm sorry, King Pelvis. I'll make the necessary preparations, but I'm saying you need to be careful."

"Spoon, by the way, Stacia's in town. Why don't you go get it?"

"Thank you, sir, but, remember, it's already been got."

"I'm wit' Donavin. I say damn deez broads. A broad wanna storm out and give all dat attitude, den git you a new broad. I say we get da three finest hoochies from da pageant which will undoubtedly be da winners 'cause it's basically an ass contest. Den we roll to da Ball lookin' like da three pretty muthafuckas dat we is and give all doze breezies a hearty beatin' up at da end of da night! A guaranteed win!"

Donavin and J.R. were on the same page. They smiled and slapped each other five. Spoon, always down for his boys, was in agreement and sealed the deal. Armed with knowledge of Stacia's arrival, he headed straight to his phone.

CHAPTER SIXTEEN

The auditorium buzzed with activity as the finishing touches were put on the show. Donavin, Spoon, and J.R. were busy directing and making executive decisions. As five o'clock approached, Donavin mingled amongst the contestants and acted as if he hadn't had a relationship meltdown the night before. He had managed to avoid Angela all afternoon, but she eventually found him.

"So," she said, batting her eyelashes, "looks like we have a date tonight."

"I have a date with the winner," Donavin returned.

"I know what I said. See ya later, honey." She kissed him lightly on the cheek, then walked away swaying her hips from side to side.

"Ooh wee, dawg." J.R. came up from behind Donavin. "Hate to see her leave, but love to watch her walk away. You gon' beat so big tonight! She's a guaranteed win. Da finest broad in da whole show."

"Do you hear that, J.R.?"

"Hear what, dawg?"

"That's the sound of her body callin' me." They gave each other a pound and laughed.

"I see you guys admiring Angela," Spoon said, approaching his friends. "Donavin, watch out, my good man. You know Jasmine is from Richmond. I think she's got a little thug in her."

"Damn a Jasmine! Oh yeah, let me tell y'all what happened last night before I picked her up from the airport. I go out to my car and who is there to greet me but Angela herself. Honey was all over me. She wants it—wants it bad. And since Jasmine's acting up, I'm gonna give it to her. Shit, I'm a playboy. I gots to get mine."

"Dawg, I'm 'bout to cry." J.R. hugged Donavin tightly. "Dat's da most sense I've heard anybody talk in my life. D, you so wise."

"'Damn a Jasmine', huh?" Spoon looked on with skepticism. "Remember those words."

"I'll be straight, Spoon. We'll be looking good, rolling in a phat stretch limo, and sporting three of the finest women this institution has to offer on our arms. Sit back and relax."

Donavin's ego swelled with confidence. He wasn't trying to convince Spoon as much as he was trying to convince himself.

The Miss Stratford Pageant went on as scheduled, and the student body was treated to quite an event. It was the normal T and A show, but it had a style and flair that had not been its trademark in previous years. By the end, as in past years, three attractive, light-skinned, long-haired beauties were named to the Court of Stratford University. Leading the way was Angela Troublefield.

All the Betas stood up and acted like fools because she was in their sister sorority. Angela basked in the spotlight with her flowers, sash, and crown. She looked absolutely radiant enjoying the spoils of her victory. After the pageant was over, Donavin approached her.

"Congratulations, Angela. I'm sure you'll have a wonderful reign." Donavin bent at the waist and gave her an exaggerated bow.

"Thank you," she replied, performing a brief curtsy. "I told you we were going to have a date tonight."

"So you did," Donavin said with a grin. "Shall we move on to the Ball?"

The BDP, along with their dates, exited the auditorium and climbed into the black Cadillac Escalade limousine.

"Spoon, you did well with the acquisition of the limo. This ride has everything," Donavin commented, looking around the vehicle.

"Hell yeah! Dis is like whoa! Jus' like my date. Whoa!" added J.R., snuggling up to the giggling second runner-up.

Aaliyah's "Rock the Boat" played softly in the background and Spoon opened the first bottle of Cristal. "This is definitely a win for the BDP." Spoon poured glasses of champagne for everyone and passed them around, then he poured a little out of the window in memory of Aaliyah.

Spoon held up his glass and said, "May we all have a night to remember."

Twenty minutes and three bottles of Cristal later, the limo pulled up to the Hyatt Regency. A crowd of alumni and students dressed in their Homecoming finery stood in the driveway to see and be seen. The BDP and Homecoming Court exited the limo on the red carpet like the royalty they were. Flashbulbs popped upon their arrival and grand entrance.

Angela was in heaven as she waved to the crowd of onlookers like she was Miss America. She had won the crown and the man. With her coup she felt poised and confident, like she was sitting on top of the world and nothing could ruin this perfect night.

The three couples posed outside of the stretch Escalade for pictures, relishing in the extra attention they received. They made their way inside the lobby and people congratulated them on a spectacular show.

A loud noise caught everyone's attention when Richard Smithers and his brothers arrived in full effect. They entered the lobby and turned it into an impromptu step show, hollering and stomping their way through the crowd. Bile rose in Donavin's throat at the site of Allen Pearson, who had obviously come back for Homecoming like many other alums. Donavin walked over and stood close to Spoon and J.R.

Donavin sucked his teeth and whispered, "Look at these sorry bastards."

"Just keep cool, guys. Let's be the gentlemen we are. However, any disrespect should be dealt with swiftly. Agreed?" Spoon scowled at the frat boys.

"It's whateva. Deez fools can git dealt wit' now far as I'm concerned. I got a whole pocket fulla ass whoopin', and I ain't afraid of handin' summa it out."

The majority of people ignored the Betas and turned their attention to the next person to enter the lobby. Keyshawn Williams stepped onto the scene wearing a gold lamé tuxedo with a top hat and cane to match. He was accompanied by a crew of some of the more flamboyant members of the Stratford community. He pranced in as if he were on a runway and proceeded to tell all the contestants how fierce they were and that they were all divas in his eyes.

"Keyshawn, the show was hella tight. I definitely want to thank you for all your hard work." Donavin reached out to shake his hand.

Keyshawn extended his hand as a woman would when she expected it to be kissed. He stepped closer to Donavin who was immediately taken aback by the advance. Flustered, confused, and slightly inebriated, Donavin missed seeing Jasmine and Stacia step out of the elevator at that moment. Angela spotted them and saw this as her opportunity to insert the final nail into the coffin Donavin and Jasmine's relationship was in.

"Excuse me, Keyshawn," Angela said, wedging herself between the two. "He's with me, Miss Thang."

Keyshawn turned on his gold shoes and muttered some curses under his breath before sashaying off with his friends in tow.

Spoon and J.R. stood to the side laughing hysterically at how Keyshawn had pushed up on Donavin.

Angela turned around to face Donavin, pressing her body firmly against his. She wrapped him in an embrace and tried to console him. While still in the embrace, she searched the crowd and did her best to make eye contact with Jasmine.

It only took about five seconds for Jasmine to see the couple and their public display of affection. The moment they caught Jasmine's attention, Angela winked at her. She then caressed the back of Donavin's head and gave him a soft, wet, passionate kiss on the neck. Donavin never really cared for such behavior in public, but he let it go because he wanted to prove his masculinity after what had just happened with Keyshawn.

At the sight of Angela kissing Donavin, anger consumed Jasmine. Stacia also noticed Angela with Donavin, but she was too late in her observations to stop Jasmine from making a beeline for them.

J.R. and Spoon were standing several yards away, still enjoying a hearty laugh at how Donavin had been approached by Keyshawn when they saw Jasmine was headed directly for their friend.

"Got dang she look mad, Spoon! Two-way dat fool Donavin and warn him."

"Oh shit! Okay."

"Donavin!" Jasmine's teeth were clenched and she was visibly angry. "We need to talk!"

Donavin's two-way went off and a message flashed across it that read, "Enemy mig on your six. Enemy mig on your six. Abort, abort!"

Donavin glanced over his shoulder at Spoon and J.R. who both stared as if he was a dead man walking.

Before he could reply to Jasmine's challenge, Angela stepped in her face. "Oh, no, you don't need to talk to him." Angela shook her head and snapped her fingers in Jasmine's face.

"This has nothing to do with you. Back up."

Angela raised her voice. "I don't know who you think you're talking to, bitch!"

With those words an interested crowd gathered to egg the two young ladies on. Stacia made her way to the front of the crowd, but did not want to get into a dispute between her friend and one of her sorors. The Betas also began to gather around the two women to see what was going on.

"Spoon, why can't you ever jus' deliver a simple ass message?" J.R. looked at the last message sent by Spoon's two-way. "All dat military code talk is too much when fools been drinkin', dawg. Dere goes Stacia's fine ass. Did you beat it up last night?"

"I surely did, Big Country." Spoon nodded.

"I'll properly congratulate you later. Let's go help dis fool."

Jasmine looked down at the floor and began to speak. "I'm a bitch, huh?" Jasmine shook her head, still looking at the floor. "*I'm* a real bitch!" she repeated, incredulously.

"Angela!" Donavin yelled. "That shit is uncalled for. Jasmine, I apolo—"

Jasmine put her opened hand to his face, effectively cutting him off. She turned around slowly, preparing to walk away from the ugly scene.

"Yeah, I thought so!" Angela rolled her neck and flung her hair over her shoulder in victory.

Jasmine stood still for a moment, clenched her fist, then spun around and unleashed a left hook to the side of Angela's face. Angela fell to the floor from the force of the blow. Cries of "Oh snap!" and "She got knocked the fuck out!" rang out through the crowd.

Jasmine removed her sequined evening shoes and diamond earrings and rushed Angela while she was still down. She slapped her across the face repeatedly until Donavin and Stacia pulled her away.

"Get off me!" Jasmine struggled to get free to inflict a few more blows.

Allen and Smithers grabbed Donavin by both of his arms as he was trying to restrain Jasmine.

"Get your fucking hands off her!" Allen demanded.

Donavin broke free with little effort and shoved Pearson down. Chaos ensued for the next few minutes. Some people pressed forward for a closer look at the action while others ran for the exits. Angela was helped out of the lobby by some of her sorority sisters, and Jasmine and Stacia fled through an emergency exit. Spoon and J.R. grabbed Donavin and took him to a corner of the lobby near the pay phones.

"I can't believe this shit! Jasmine thinks she's Mike fuckin' Tyson and that piece of shit Pearson put his muthafuckin' hands on me!" Donavin paced angrily like a caged animal.

"Hey, dawg. Y'all my boys. I say we stomp some Beta asses and git da hell on befo' da police git here." J.R. cracked his knuckles and did some quick stretches to loosen up his muscles.

Spoon shook his head that it had come to this. "This was inevitable, I suppose. Damn, I look too pretty tonight to get into a street fight. All I know is nobody better hit me in my face. Oh well, just fight as hard as you can and get back to the limo."

The BDP took their jackets off and turned to walk back into the main foyer of the lobby. Ten Beta Alpha Delta brothers surrounded them.

"You should have never put your hands on me, bitch," Allen said, his confidence buoyed now that his crew was behind him.

Donavin responded in kind. "You've already seen what happens to people who call other people bitch."

The BDP stood together steadfast. There was no fear in any of them for they honestly believed that they could win, even with the cards so heavily stacked against them.

J.R. was ready to get it on and decided to instigate more conflict. "Look at dis collection of sorry summumma bitches. I think we'll whoop each and every one a y'all ignant asses, den I'll go to da liquor sto' and me and my boys are gon' git absolutely toasted while talkin' shit 'bout how we stomped yo' asses into da ground. Need I say mo'?"

Laughter rang out among the onlookers and the Betas converged on the BDP. Donavin, Spoon, and J.R. shifted into survival-of-the-fittest mode. One by one, the BDP began to dispose of the Betas. J.R. looked as if he were enjoying himself as he delivered blow after blow. Donavin and Spoon stood back to back and put down all comers. The fighting ended rather quickly and the BDP remained the only combatants left standing. J.R. and Spoon headed toward the door.

J.R. called after Donavin, who lagged behind to take a few more shots at some of the Betas still exhibiting signs of consciousness. "Dawg, come yo' black ass on befo' we git hemmed up by da police!"

Donavin was about to flee, but Allen got up and challenged him once more. Allen, who had been the recipient of a J.R. special, was visibly shaken but still had a little fight left in him. He rushed Donavin from behind as he was running to join his friends. Allen gave him a cheap shot in the back. Donavin stumbled forward, but regained his balance.

"Come on!" Allen screamed.

Donavin gave him a cold, hard stare. He stood perfectly still and then raised his fists to defend himself. Allen swung at him wildly, but Donavin blocked it downward and came back with an elbow to Allen's face. Allen fell backward and his nose began to bleed profusely.

"Get up, muthafucka!" Donavin taunted, standing over Allen like Ali stood over Frazier. Allen remained on the floor, writhing in pain.

"Come da fuck on!" J.R. pleaded.

Donavin ran for the exit door and leapt into the awaiting limousine. The driver sped off before Donavin could close the door.

CHAPTER SEVENTEEN

"I'm a fuckin' killa! I'm harder dan da muthafuckin' Gladiator! I was straight handlin' fools!" J.R. bragged about his performance as he strutted around the apartment in a wifebeater tank top. "Man! I hope nobody ever whoops my ass da way I was whoopin' fools tonight!"

"Yeah, son!" Donavin punched J.R. in the chest. "From now on, that's how we handle shit! Did you see how I knocked Pearson the fuck out?" Donavin took a pillow from the couch and reenacted the knockout blow from earlier. "I hope he hasn't learned his lesson. Matter of fact, I hope he tries his luck again. Next time it'll be sad singin' and casket bringin' out this muthafucka!"

"You a killa, too, dawg! Hold up." J.R. went to his room and came back with a baseball bat. "I say we find dem fools and finish da shit. What's up?"

"Let's do it!" Donavin agreed.

Spoon was the coolest of the bunch and he decided to interject before Donavin and J.R. went looking for more trouble. "Fellas, calm down! It's over. Let's just be cool. Sit down, relax, and watch some TV."

"We ain't gon' go out and whoop some mo' asses?" J.R. asked.

"No, J.R., no more ass whoopin's today." Spoon's even voice and demeanor defused the testosterone in the room.

Donavin listened to Spoon's reasoning. "Yeah, we should just chill and lay low for the rest of the weekend. I'll call Winston and he'll coordinate with our committees to make sure that the other events are cool."

The BDP grabbed some refreshments from the kitchen and began to watch television.

"Tonight a near riot broke out at the Hyatt Regency in downtown Atlanta during the Stratford University Homecoming festivities. The full story is coming up at eleven on Eyewitness News."

All of them put their heads down and said "Damn" in unison.

A few minutes later, the phone rang and Donavin answered.

"Mr. Jackson!" A stern voice lashed at him. "I don't like to hear that the president of my student body is out starting fights like some common street thug," said Dean Edwards, Dean of Student Affairs. Contempt filled his voice. "You and your friends have embarrassed my institution and I will not stand for it. There will be a hearing on this matter at ten A.M. Monday morning. Don't worry about missing any classes. Very soon you may not have to worry about class at all. Good evening to you."

Donavin hung up without a reply and sighed. "Dean Edwards is going to try to have us expelled from school on Monday morning, boys."

Spoon raised an eyebrow. "Well, that's not too cool at all."

J.R. responded with less levity. "Man! My momma gon' kick my ass if I git kicked outta school. We gots to come up wit' a plan quick!"

"It was three on ten," Donavin stated. "There's no way anyone could possibly blame us. This hearing will be a cakewalk."

Spoon didn't share Donavin's cavalier attitude. "You sure are confident. Are you forgetting that Dean Edwards is an old school

Beta? We have to come up with something big not to lose on this one. I, for one, don't know what it is. Oh well, I'm going to bed." Spoon got up and walked to his room looking dejected and tired.

"Hey, dawg," J.R. said mildly. "On Monday we jus' gotta go up in dere and git it how we live. Whateva happens, happens. I'm gon' go fall into a coma now. I'll holla at you in the mornin'. Peace." J.R. went to his room to get some sleep as well.

Donavin sat alone wondering how things had gone so wrong so quickly. He wished that he had never gotten into a fight with Jasmine. He wished that he had stopped the fight between Angela and Jasmine. He wished that he had walked away from the altercation with the Betas. Nah, he didn't wish the last one.

Sitting back in the armchair, he was about to doze off when there was a knock at the door. He got up and looked through the peephole to see Jasmine on the other side. She was wearing an Ace bandage around her wrist.

Donavin opened the door and folded his arms across his chest. "Jasmine." Donavin greeted her in a monotone voice, then turned his back on her and sat back down.

"Nice to see you, too." She entered and closed the door behind her.

"Look, I just had to fight my way out of a hotel and ride away in a getaway car like I'm a damned rapper or something. And, oh yeah, I just got a call from the Dean. They're going to try to expel our asses on Monday."

"Oh my God. I'm sorry. I lost control, but that girl had it coming with that mouth of hers. You should've told me about what was going on between the two of you. I would have respected it and left you alone."

"You obviously saw her kissing my neck. That was wrong, but I let it go because Keyshawn Williams was trying to hit on me. I just wanted people to know that I'm very much hetero."

"Everyone already knows that, believe me. Even before tonight, I've been hearing that you and Angela were becoming quite the couple."

"That's bullshit, Jas. We should have just talked about it calmly and avoided all the drama. Instead you kept listening to Stacia and the rest of the fucking peanut gallery. Angela was wrong to say what she said, but you can't start a fight every time someone calls you out of your name. That's just fucking childish."

"Well, I simply wanted to say that I'm sorry for the situation. *Not* the way I reacted. But I'm glad to see you're okay. I had to make my own getaway. I heard that you guys handled yourselves pretty well. You so strong." She mocked him by feeling on his bicep.

Donavin cracked a smile. "Ugh . . . this is so messed up."

Jasmine smiled back and asked, "What can I do to help?"

"You've done enough already, trust me." Donavin was testy with her again.

"I said I was sorry!" Jasmine returned fire. "Your little friend's mouth writes checks her ass can't cash."

"To go over covered material once again, whom I associate with is not your business."

Donavin's arrogance infuriated Jasmine. "You know what!" Jasmine's eyes began to water and she raised her voice. "You keep your little light-skinned Gamma Ray-looking bitch 'cause I have absolutely no use for you."

"Jasmine, lower your voice," Donavin said, annoyed. He began to get up.

"Don't get up, muthafucka!" Jasmine stood over him threateningly. "I'm from Richmond, and I already knocked one bitch out tonight."

Donavin sat back down because he didn't want to get into another fight, especially not with a woman. "I'm not having this conversation with you right now." He leaned back and began to flick the channels with the remote control.

"Okay, fine. I'm just going to use the bathroom then I'll be out of your way."

Donavin ignored her and focused solely on the television. She came back a few minutes later with the bathroom trash can filled to the brim with water. Before Donavin could react, she dashed the cold water on him, then ran out the door. Spoon and J.R. came out of their rooms to see what all the commotion was and laughed boisterously at Donavin's new wet look.

As the water soaked his clothes and favorite chair, Donavin sat in disbelief for a few stunned seconds before he went after her.

"Are you fucking crazy?" Donavin cursed at Jasmine who was now behind the wheel of her rental car. "Get your ass out of the car now," he commanded.

Jasmine did the opposite. She gave him the finger, turned the ignition, and put the car in reverse. Donavin jumped onto the hood while the car lurched backwards. This didn't deter Jasmine. She put the car in drive with Donavin still sprawled across the hood.

J.R. and Spoon came running from the apartment. Instead of imploring Jasmine to stop, they simply laughed harder at the bizarre sight of Donavin clinging to the hood of a car going about fifty miles an hour.

"Dat fool 'bout to git it if he fall off dat hood." J.R. gasped for air.

By now, Jasmine could not see through the sea of tears that streamed down her face.

"If you don't stop this car!" Donavin threatened as Jasmine turned on the windshield wipers.

At speeds that began to approach seventy miles per hour, Donavin recognized her resolve. He held on as she hit the gas, speeding down the streets of the apartment complex. She eventually slowed down and came to a stop. Jasmine rolled down the window and cried out, "You have two seconds to get your ass off this car." Donavin did as she said and Jasmine sped off.

Nearly ten minutes later, Donavin's heart was still pounding against his chest from the ride he had just taken. Finally reaching the apartment, he wanted only to get into his bed and forget that this day ever happened.

As he entered the apartment, he found J.R. and Spoon in the living room sitting quietly. At the sight of Donavin drenched in water, wiper fluid, and sweat wearing a look as if he was ready to kill, J.R. and Spoon struggled to keep straight faces, but the situation was simply too comical to them.

"Man, did you see dis fool on top of da hood tryna be Wesley Snipes Passenger 58 and shit?" J.R. opened up on his friend.

Spoon took a jab as well. "And the award for Stunt Negro of the Year goes to Donavin Action Jackson!"

"Dawg," J.R. began, sitting back on the sofa, "no piece of ass is worth dyin' over. You crazy fuh jumpin' on dat broad's hood."

Even Donavin had to laugh. "That was some dumb shit, huh?"

"Hell yeah!" J.R. said loudly.

"This has been the night from hell."

"Oh yeah, D, your mom just called and said for you to call her," Spoon informed him.

"You didn't tell her what happened, did you?"

"No, I just said that you went for a ride." Spoon could barely finish his statement without cracking up. J.R. joined him.

"Ha fucking ha. I'll have to call her later. I can't deal right now. I'm going to bed before some more crazy shit happens." Donavin said goodnight to his friends and fell asleep almost as soon as his head hit the pillow.

CHAPTER EIGHTEEN

Donavin, Spoon, and J.R. gathered around the kitchen table Monday morning to prepare themselves.

"Well, boys, looks like we're in a little bit of trouble, and soon we'll find out just how much."

"This is true, Donavin," Spoon answered. "All we can do is explain what happened and appeal to the Dean's sense of fairness."

"Y'all is trippin'. Dean Edwards is such a Beta. We gon' need a act of God to keep us from gittin' kicked out. Matter of fact, I say we pray."

J.R. went for his Bible and returned shortly to lead them in prayer. "Lawd God, I know we so undeservin', but please, Lawd, don't let us git expelled from school today. Lead us away from da dark side and toward da light and da love of Yo' son, Jesus." J.R. began to feel the Spirit move within him. "Yes Lawd!" He threw up his hands. "Give us da strength to face our accusers . . . Ha! Let us bask in da glory of Yo' love . . . Ha! Help us put da devil on da run, Lawd . . . Ha! Help us rebuke da evil spirits, Lawd . . . Ha!"

"Preach on, preach on," Spoon encouraged.

"In Yo' son, Jesus' name we pray fuh a blessin'."

They said amen and hugged each other like the brothers they

were. All three felt sufficiently energized by putting their fate in God's hands.

They arrived on campus at about fifteen minutes to ten and each knew that it was showtime. They were immaculately groomed and dressed in their finest business suits. The campus audience began to buzz as they walked through the Quad on their way to Killington Hall. The prospect of the three most powerful and respected students on campus being kicked out of school made for great gossip. Each of them walked toward the building with his game face on.

By the time they got to Killington Hall a crowd had begun to form. It was almost similar to when people gathered to hear the verdict of the O.J. trial. The mood was pensive and no one spoke to them. They only whispered and pointed. Donavin reached the door first and opened it for Spoon and J.R. They turned the corner and entered the elevator that would take them upstairs to where the hearing was to be held.

"Let's just be calm and explain what happened. We'll apologize for any negative reflection on the school and be gentlemen about the whole ordeal." Spoon straightened his tie.

"I don't know about an apology," replied Donavin. "Three on ten is hardly a fair fight. They should apologize to us."

"Leave the attitude on the elevator, D," Spoon implored.

"Dis is some fuckin' bullshit." J.R. was frustrated. "How we gon' git in trouble fuh fightin' ten dudes? I should be congratulated fuh whoopin' ten grown ass men!"

"And you don't get to talk in there, Big Country," Spoon shot back.

The elevator reached the top floor and the Dean intercepted them within two steps of their exiting.

"Sit in the conference room around the corner," Dean Edwards commanded. "We'll be with you momentarily." He turned and went the opposite way to his private office.

"We?" J.R. questioned. "Who da hell is we?"

"Come on, Big Country." Donavin put his hand on J.R.'s shoulder and guided him into the conference room.

They entered the room and sat down. Moments later, they looked up to see a parade of Beta Alpha Delta men entering the room. Donavin, Spoon and J.R. were shocked to see the same Betas—minus Allen—with whom they had fought on Friday night come into the room bandaged up. One even limped in on crutches. At the tail end of the line came Dean Edwards and Richard Smithers who were both smiling from ear to ear. Smithers wore a large Band-Aid over his left eye.

Donavin returned the smile to hide the fact that he had a sinking feeling in his stomach that he and his friends were being set up.

After he seated himself, Dean Edwards began the proceedings. "Jackson, explain." He then withdrew an hourglass from his pocket and turned it upside down to metaphorically show Donavin that his time was running out.

"Yes, sir, I'll begin," Donavin returned calmly. "An altercation broke out between two young ladies that a few of us know in common. I tried to break it up, and my friends and I were attacked by the young men sitting in this room who happen to be Betas. It was all a big misunderstanding, and I'm sure that all parties concerned are very disappointed in what took place."

"The smugness of your attitude repulses me." Dean Edwards laid into Donavin. "How dare you start a brawl like a common street thug and embarrass this university? These young men told me all about what you call an attack. Your jealousy over the solidarity of the Beta Alpha Delta bond is deplorable and despicable. Some student government president you are. From what I understand you savagely attacked some of my young brothers from behind, and some of their brothers came to their aid. You three are cowards!"

"We just took on all ten of 'em, huh?" J.R. countered.

"That's enough out of you!" Dean Edwards snapped.

"Dean," Spoon spoke softly to try to calm everyone's flaring tempers. "What J.R. is trying to say is that we are but three. How could we have started a fight with ten individuals?"

"I've heard enough. I recommend expulsion effective immediately." Dean Edwards was obstinate. "Those colossal egos have finally landed you in a jam that there is no way out of. And furthermore—"

"Hold on just a second!" Donavin's father strode into the room.

Donavin, Spoon, and J.R.'s eyes widened one by one at the sight of Donavin's dad.

"These proceedings are restricted to Stratford University personnel only." The Dean rose from his chair in protest.

"Save it, Philip," answered Mr. Jackson.

Donavin's mouth hung open. *Philip? Don't even tell me this is the same cat my pops had beef with back in the day. You mean this clown was trying trying to get with my momma? Oh God!*

"Philip, I happen to have obtained the security videotape from the night in question. It's plain to see that my son and his friends were not the instigators. It looks to me like your guys bit off a little more than they could chew."

Mr. Jackson walked over to the television in the corner and inserted the tape into the VCR beneath it. As the tape played, a look of shame and embarrassment came over the faces of the Betas, including Dean Edwards. The Dean began to grit his teeth and tremble nervously. The evidence was irrefutable and unmistakable.

The Dean spoke in almost a whisper. "In light of this new evidence, the charges are dismissed."

"Boys, go to class." Mr. Jackson shot a long glance at his son and his friends. They filed out, but the Betas remained. Mr. Jackson looked at the student Betas and reiterated his last statement. "'Boys' includes you all as well. I don't want to have to repeat myself."

They did as he said, each of them nearly falling over the next as they scurried toward the door. Dean Edwards and Mr. Jackson were now alone. Face to face. Man to man.

"Philip, whatever our differences have been in the past, they have been between you and me. I can't believe that you had the audacity to try to railroad my son like this, in a hearing that his parents were not notified of no less." He stepped closer to Dean Edwards and leaned forward to make his point. "Let me help you understand. If you ever so much as look at my kid the wrong way again, I'll spend the rest of my days making your existence more miserable than it already is. Are we clear?"

The Dean sat with his teeth clenched.

"I'll take your silence as compliance. Take it easy, Philip." Mr. Jackson sarcastically patted him on the back and exited the conference room. He took the elevator downstairs and was met on the steps by nearly the entire student body who began to cheer at the sight of him. The BDP had already told everyone what had happened during the hearing. At the front of the crowd were Donavin, J.R., and Spoon, who had defied Mr. Jackson's order to go to class.

J.R. expressed his joy as only he could. "What you jus' did was way pimpish, Mr. Jackson."

They all laughed and began to move through the crowd. It was quite striking to see Donavin walk with his father. To look at Congressman Jackson was to look at Donavin in twenty-five years. Mr. Jackson sought private audience with the young men on a bench in front of the Science Department.

"Donavin, I'm very disappointed that you didn't call us," Mr. Jackson began. "When something like this happens, you call your parents first. We're here to protect you. That was really dumb to walk into that hearing empty-handed. And you call yourselves the Billion Dollar Playboys? Not quite yet. I think you guys might still be in the thousands."

Mr. Jackson smiled and patted Spoon and J.R. on their backs. "If you gentlemen will excuse us, let me talk to my son for a few minutes."

Spoon and J.R. thanked Mr. Jackson and walked away, leaving Donavin alone with his father.

"What's up, Pop?" Donavin asked.

"You know I don't mince words, and we've spared you long enough. Your mom has been undergoing chemotherapy for stomach cancer over the last couple of months, and she's not doing well at all. We were hoping that she would have a quick recovery, and we wouldn't have to share this with you."

The joy drained from Donavin's face and was replaced by concern and hurt.

Mr. Jackson smiled slightly and said, "Don't go digging her grave just yet. She's had to stop teaching, but she's a tough lady. We just thought that you should know so it doesn't come as a complete shock."

"Damn," Donavin said in disbelief. "I gotta go home and see her."

Donavin's dad shook his head. "No, you need to stay here and graduate. Everything will be okay. Just do your thing here and come home for Thanksgiving. It's only a few weeks away."

Donavin nodded his head. "Pop, how did you know that we were in trouble?"

"Your girlfriend, Jasmine, did what you should have done. She called me."

"She is *not* my girlfriend. She's just a crazy female like all the rest of 'em."

"Maybe she's just crazy about you. That's the way love goes sometimes, kid."

Donavin stared off for a few moments, digesting everything that his father had told him.

Mr. Jackson stood. "Donavin, I've got to get back to Washington. Everything will be okay, I promise. I love you, son."

Donavin stood and hugged his father half-heartedly. "I love you, too, Pop."

After the embrace Mr. Jackson left Donavin alone on the bench to think about the state of things. His mother being sick was something he could not begin to fathom.

And he could not help but think about how Jasmine had indirectly saved him in his time of need.

CHAPTER NINETEEN

Thanksgiving break came, and Donavin could hardly hide his anxiousness to see his mother. His father insisted that he concentrate on his studies since learning the news instead of flying up every weekend to visit her like he wanted to. He left on a flight to New Jersey that Wednesday night and was met by a grim-looking, sleep-deprived Mr. Jackson at the baggage claim of Newark International Airport. Donavin had never seen his father look so exhausted and solemn.

"What's wrong?" Donavin feared the answer.

Mr. Jackson forced a smile to put his son at ease. "It's your mom. She's taken a turn for the worse. She's weak, and she's lost a lot of weight. I think it will raise her spirits to see you."

They retrieved the luggage and drove in silence directly to the Rahway Regional Cancer Center. Visiting hours were nearly over, and the nurse told them that they had little time to spend with her. Donavin stepped into his mother's private room and felt lightheaded at the sight of her.

Most of her beautiful long hair had fallen out due to the chemotherapy, and it appeared she'd lost nearly half of her body weight. Her physical appearance had deteriorated in the three months since he had last seen her.

"Donny." Mrs. Jackson smiled weakly at the sight of her only child.

Donavin rushed to her side and hugged her tightly. Tears welled in his eyes as he gazed upon the woman who had been a pillar of strength to him all of his life.

"Hey, Momma. I love you." He grabbed her hand.

"Donny . . ." Mrs. Jackson barely had the strength to speak. "I think that God is going to take me home soon. I want the both of you to listen to me now." Donavin's dad drew closer to the bed and stroked his wife's forehead. "My life is about this family. I've watched both of you grow from boys into beautiful, strong, independent black men. I'm thankful for having been a wife and a mother. I wish I didn't have to leave you guys so soon, but there's nothing we can do about that. Just know that the love I have in my heart for both of you will never die."

Mr. Jackson fought back tears and took hold of his wife's other hand. Donavin couldn't hold back any longer and began to cry. He had never encountered anything in his life that he couldn't best or somehow overcome. Now it just seemed like a matter of time before his mother would succumb to her illness, and he was unable to do anything to change the course of her fate. A few minutes of silence ensued with Donavin and his father staring at her and clutching her hands. Then her grip loosened and a single tear ran down her cheek.

Mr. Jackson was the first to notice that she was flatlining. Donavin was oblivious to it and held on to her as if he could somehow save her if he just didn't let go.

Doctors and nurses rushed the room and it took three orderlies to remove Donavin. The doctors emerged from her room and spoke to Mr. Jackson.

Donavin waited alone in the waiting room, but he could see the doctors talking to his father. When he saw his father put his head down after talking to the doctors, he knew that his mother was gone. The tears flowed from his eyes once again, but he didn't make a sound or say a word.

His father entered the waiting room and hugged him. Mr. Jackson was stoic; Donavin was amazed by his father's strength. The two of them never imagined a future without Mrs. Jackson. Now they faced an uncertain one together.

The men left the hospital after one A.M. to make the lonely drive home. Donavin and his father again rode in silence. Neither knew what to say to the other. Normally both were very eloquent; now they were at a total loss for words.

When they arrived at the house, Donavin went upstairs to his room and shut the door. He lay down fully clothed on top of his comforter and buried his head in the pillow. The ringing of his cell phone caught his attention.

"Donavin, is everything okay? How is your mom?" Spoon asked.

Hearing her referred to as if she was still alive crushed Donavin. "Man." Donavin tried to hold it together. "I . . . I was just with her when she passed a couple of hours ago."

"Oh my God. Look, I'm at home. I'm leaving now. I'll be there in a little over an hour."

"Thanks, man."

Donavin's phone beeped from another incoming call.

"I'll see you soon." Donavin answered the other line wearily, "Hello."

"Hey, dawg. Somethin' told me to check up on ya. How's Momma Jackson holdin' up?"

Another dagger pierced Donavin's heart. He quietly replied, "She passed a little earlier."

J.R. groaned. "Dawg, I'm so sorry, man. I . . . don't . . . oh, neva mind. I'm at home in New Orleans, but I'm on da first thang smokin' in da mornin'. I'll see you tomorrow. Keep ya head up, D. Yo' momma's wit' God now. I'll pray fuh yo' family."

Donavin disconnected the call and threw his cell phone and two-way across the room. They bounced on the carpet and landed in the corner.

Pray. Yeah, right. I don't want Momma with God. I want her with me.
His tears began anew.

The next morning Donavin sat at the kitchen table with Spoon who, true to his word, arrived at the house approximately an hour after their phone call. Shortly after nine there was a knock at the door, and J.R. walked in from the first flight that morning. J.R. immediately bear-hugged Donavin and began to cry. He was not one to hide his emotions. Donavin, on the other hand, remained unemotional, maintaining his composure.

"Okay," J.R. said, trying to pull himself together. He reached into his backpack. "I brought my Bible, man. Let's git our prayer on."

"I don't think that's going to happen. I control my destiny, not Him." Donavin pointed toward the sky in defiance.

"Whoa!" Spoon said. He and J.R. stepped away from Donavin as if he were about to be struck by lightning.

"Man, is you too dumb to know dat God is testin' you, dawg? Da devil wants you to turn from God. Don't be Anakin Skywalker, be Luke. When dat man, Anakin, was confronted wit' a choice, he chose evil. Den he became Darth Vader who was just a playa hater, dawg. Be Luke, man. Choose love. Rebuke da hate."

"Wow!" Spoon was astonished. "You never cease to amaze me. That wildly drawn out analogy actually made some sense. I think I just learned some new existential shit."

145

"Be that as it may." Donavin was stern. "You can take all that prayin' and shit outside. God can stay out of my shit and I'll stay out of His."

J.R. tried to reason further. "Bruh—"

"Give him some time," Spoon interrupted. "Where's your father, D?"

"In his room, I guess. I haven't seen him since we came back last night."

"Let's go check on him," said Spoon.

They walked up the stairs, and Donavin knocked on the door to his parents' bedroom.

"Come in."

Donavin opened the door and saw a sight that he had never seen before nor ever expected to see. His father sat in the middle of the floor weeping. Scattered around him were old photo albums and other memorabilia that chronicled his life with Vanessa. Oldies played softly in the background from the stereo.

Mr. Jackson cleared his throat and smiled at the sight of Spoon and J.R. "Good morning, boys." Mr. Jackson motioned to them with his hand. "Take a look." He cleared a space and Donavin, Spoon, and J.R. took seats next to him.

Donavin had never seen many of these pictures before. They seemed to go in order from when his parents first met at Stratford all the way to the present. In looking at the pictures, Donavin and his father shared a sense of joy in remembering Vanessa.

"Got dang, yo' afro was big, Mr. Jackson," said J.R. "It looked like you was tryna hide Buckwheat on top o' yo' head."

Everyone, including Donavin, laughed. They looked at the pictures for the remainder of the morning until J.R.'s stomach growled loud enough for everyone to hear.

"Y'all, it's Thanksgiving Day, and we ain't got no food. I guess we can be thankful dat we at least together today."

"That we can," agreed Mr. Jackson.

"I'm sure my parents would be more than happy to accommodate us. Let me ring them to make sure." Spoon reached into his pocket for his cell phone.

"I don't know, dawg. Y'all bougie black folks be cookin' some wild stuff. I ain't tryna eat no collard green soufflé."

Everyone laughed heartily at J.R.'s silliness. Donavin's cell phone rang and interrupted his laughter.

"Hello." There was a short silence and then he heard a sniffle.

"Oh, Brown Eyes," Jasmine began. "I had no idea about your mom. I'm so sorry. I know you must be going through hell right now."

Donavin put on his tough guy demeanor, but his heart jumped at the sound of her voice. "Hey Jas, thanks for calling, but I'm okay. It's just one of those things that couldn't be helped. Why aren't you in Richmond?"

"I was getting ready to take an early train down when Spoon called me this morning. It's Thanksgiving. I know you guys must not have any food. Do you mind if Stacia and I come over and cook for you?"

"Thanks, Baby Girl. That would be the bomb," Donavin said, remembering her culinary skills. He paused briefly. "I've missed you."

"Me too," she said.

Almost immediately after Donavin got off the phone with Jasmine, the calls began coming one after the other with people offering their condolences to the family. Donavin let his father handle the phone calls because he began to feel great sadness over the fact that he would never see his mother again. A few hours after he spoke to her, Jasmine showed up with Stacia and several bags full of groceries.

As soon as she'd entered the front door, Jasmine ran to Donavin and threw her arms around him. She hugged him long and hard.

"I'm so sorry for your loss, Brown Eyes."

"Thanks, Baby Girl. It's good to see you." He clutched her tightly as if he never wanted to let her go.

"I've missed you so much. I'm sorry I tried to run you over last month." She looked up at him with adoring eyes and then kissed his lips.

"It's cool. I can put it on my resume if I ever decide to start making action flicks."

"S'up, Speed Racer." J.R greeted Jasmine as he came into the foyer. Spoon followed closely behind.

"Hey, slugger." Spoon winked at Jasmine and moved in closer to give Stacia a hug.

"Hey, where y'all girl at?" J.R. asked Stacia as he took the bags from her hands.

"Carmen will be here in a little while. She's just running a little late, Big Boy," answered Stacia.

"She's bringing a turkey from her mother's house in the Bronx. We're gonna throw down on the side dishes, though. Come on, let's do this, girl." Jasmine turned to Stacia and the two headed to the kitchen.

The scene was very surreal to Donavin. He had expected to spend Thanksgiving with his mother and father, and now all of these outside people were there. Mr. Jackson put on some more oldies, and everyone seemed to unwind as the music of Marvin Gaye and Teddy Pendergrass began to fill the air. The air was soon filled with the aroma of macaroni and cheese, candied yams, cornbread stuffing, and collard greens. At around five-thirty, much to J.R.'s delight, Carmen arrived with the turkey.

Donavin was amazed by the fact that all of his friends had chosen to spend Thanksgiving away from their families with him and his father. As a matter of fact, he felt guilty about it. One, for all of them just being there, and two, because his mother hadn't been gone for twenty-four hours and he was having a good time with his company.

At dinnertime, everyone sat down at the dining room table ready for the impromptu feast. "Let us bow our heads," Mr. Jackson began.

Donavin balled up his napkin, threw it on the floor, and stormed away from the table. Mr. Jackson stood up quickly and summoned his son back to the table. "Boy, get back here. What's the matter with you?"

"I'm not praying to a God who doesn't listen to prayers," Donavin replied angrily.

Mr. Jackson was compassionate. "I know you're upset, son, and in time you'll come to terms with your relationship with the Lord. But you're not upset with your mother, so take this time to say something to her."

Donavin stood still, staring at the floor. Jasmine arose from her seat, took him by the hand, and led him back to the table.

He sat back down, closed his eyes, and began to speak to his mother. "Mom, I don't know what to say." He lifted his face toward heaven. "You were and are such an important part of my life and now you're not here anymore. I loved you, but I didn't appreciate you the way that I should have. I wasn't . . . I wasn't . . . " He faltered, fighting back tears. Jasmine rubbed his arm. "I wasn't the best son to you that I could have been, but I'm going to do the best I can to prove my love to your memory. I love you, Momma. I'll never forget you."

Not one eye remained dry. An outpouring of emotion rose from the table.

Mr. Jackson raised his glass. "Eloquently said, my son, but you were in no way a disappointment. Your mother loved you because of the man you've become."

That Saturday they buried Mrs. Jackson in a beautiful ceremony that was attended by hundreds of people. Jasmine, Spoon, and J.R. never left Donavin's side.

CHAPTER
TWENTY

The BDP took a flight back to Atlanta early Monday morning. From the moment they arrived on campus, people approached Donavin offering condolences over his loss. Winston was one of the first to approach.

"Donavin, man, I'm so sorry." He tried to give Donavin some dap but was stopped halfway.

"I'm cool," Donavin said, shaking his head. "I'll be all right."

"If there's anything I can do, D, you just let me know."

"Thanks, man."

To Donavin, everything seemed to move in slow motion. His once stable existence had become an absolute mess. He was fighting in public, had almost been kicked out of school, and his mother had passed. Senior year was definitely not shaping up according to plan.

"Donavin," a familiar voice called out as he walked to class. It was Angela. She ran to him and held him tightly.

J.R whispered to Spoon, "Man, if dat broad ever grabbed my shit like dat. I would beat 'til somebody passed da fuck out."

"You're so strong coming back to school so soon." Angela looked at Donavin with genuine sorrow.

He backed away slightly. "I'm cool. I just need to finish up the semester then the year. School will help keep my mind off things."

"Well, if you need anything or just want to talk, call me."

"Yeah, I'll do that, Ange. Don't be late for class. I'll talk to you later." Donavin dismissed her.

She walked away and J.R. and Spoon let loose.

"Dat breezie's drawers git moist every time she see yo' ignant ass. Please tap dat fuh da bruthas please," J.R. pleaded with Donavin.

"I think I'm just going to chill," Donavin replied. "Me and Jasmine seem to be in a cool place right now."

"Right now being the operative words," Spoon chimed in. "There's no reason why you shouldn't have both."

"Spoon, you a genius. Dat's da smartest thang I've heard you say in my life."

"Fellas, I don't feel much like doing anything or anyone right now." With that, Donavin looked at the ground and made his way to class.

For the remaining week and a half of the semester, Donavin was distracted and couldn't keep his mind on his books. Because everyone kept telling him how sorry they were all the time, he missed his mother desperately and began to sink into depression. Jasmine called him daily to check on him, but he needed someone to be closer. Then there was Angela, who made herself more than available to talk whenever he needed her.

After finals were over, most people were celebrating the end of the semester. Donavin, however, dreaded having to go home for the winter break to endure his first Christmas without his mother. He was feeling lonely and decided to give Angela a call, but her room-mate picked up.

"What's up, this is Donavin. Is Angela around?"

"Um . . . um," her roommate faltered. "She's in the shower."

Donavin sensed she was hiding something. "Okay, I'll talk to her later." His curiosity got the best of him, so he grabbed a jacket and got into his car. Within minutes he was at her apartment complex to see what was really going on.

He drove into her complex and killed the headlights about fifty yards from her apartment. He let the car roll a little closer and then spotted Angela with a rather tall gentleman walking toward a white Bentley. Donavin rolled forward to get a closer look and recognized Jamal Davis, a power forward for the Hawks. As Jamal opened the door for Angela, he bent down to kiss her. Angela kissed him hungrily and reached into his sweatpants, then sat in the car and kissed him hungrily below the belt.

Donavin laughed halfheartedly, put the car in reverse, and drove away undetected. He felt torn. On one hand, he was feeling jealous because he was supposed to have all the girls; on the other, he was glad to have irrefutable evidence that Angela would get with any brother with a nice-sized bank account.

Donavin turned up the radio as loud as it would go and hit the gas. With his speed rapidly approaching ninety miles per hour, he drove down Peachtree Street in search of a liquor store. He found one on the corner of Collier and Peachtree. Inside the store, he went straight for the vodka, then the orange juice. In the parking lot, he emptied half the glass container of orange juice and replenished it with half the bottle of vodka. He threw the remainder of what was left in the bottle of vodka in the trunk.

He shook the bottle to mix its contents as he sped away. Once behind the wheel of the car, Donavin took swig after swig of his makeshift Screwdriver. He thought about how every year of his life had been so perfect until this one. After a while, he got drowsy and a little tipsy, so he decided to call it a night before he got pulled over or wrapped the car around a tree.

When he entered his apartment, Spoon and J.R. were up watching television.

"You guys will never guess who I saw," Donavin slurred.

"Dawg, how 'bout I un-guess. How 'bout dat?" J.R. answered.

Donavin ignored the smart answer and said, "Jamal Davis."

"Dat man can hoop," J.R. responded. "He was a straight beast in da playoffs befo' New York knocked 'em out last season. Where you see dat fool at?"

"Over at Angela's apartment complex. She was giving him head in his Bentley," Donavin replied.

"Beep, beep, beep!" J.R. cried out.

"What are you doing, J.R.?" Spoon asked confused.

"Dat's my skeeza alert. It starts goin' off when gold diggin' tramps is around. D, I say you beat it up anyway. Dis jus' takes da pressha off you. Now you really know she ain't 'bout shit, so you might as well bust dat good nut." J.R. was brutally honest as usual.

"Once again, I'm floored by the ignorance of your reasoning," Spoon said. "You're so ignorant, yet you make perfect sense."

J.R. cocked his head in Spoon's direction. "Why . . . I don't know whether to thank you or hit you in yo' jaw?"

"The Spoon says that you should hit it for hitting sake. If she acts crazy or starts telling her friends, then simply threaten to tell about how you saw her with Kobe Bryant."

"Jamal Davis," Donavin corrected.

"Whatever. I knew it was one of those six-nine ball-playing Negroes." Spoon laughed.

"I'm gonna go make another drink." Donavin started to walk to the liquor cabinet in the kitchen.

Spoon and J.R. both looked at each other and raised their eyebrows.

Donavin went to the liquor cabinet, made himself another drink and went to his room.

"J.R., Donavin's been drinking a lot of alcohol lately. I understand things have to be hard on the guy right now, but damn,"

Spoon said, his concern evident in his voice.

"Dawg, he jus' gotta work his way through it, dat's all. D will git back to normal. You know he was a momma's boy. He'll be aight."

"My concern is that he's going home tomorrow. At least school can be a distraction. Imagine Christmas without your mom."

"Damn, dawg. I almost forgot it's Christmas time." J.R. dropped his head and sighed deeply.

CHAPTER TWENTY-ONE

Christmas came and went with Donavin falling deeper into depression. Each day his drinking grew increasingly out of hand and the wall he'd built around himself—the wall that most notably excluded Jasmine and his father—grew taller. He missed his mother and didn't know how to deal with her passing.

The Friday after Christmas, Spoon gave Donavin a call to try to get him out of the house.

"Hey, Donavin, how are you holding up?"

"I'm maintainin'."

"Just maintaining? That doesn't sound too good. How's your dad doing?"

"I don't know. He's been out of town a lot. I haven't really spoken to him."

"You're alone?"

"Yeah."

"D, you gotta come out with me tonight. Staying in your room all day avoiding your friends isn't cool."

"I'm straight, Spoon. Maybe another time," Donavin said under his breath, barely audible enough for Spoon to hear.

"Listen, a couple of guys that graduated from Stratford are having a party at Metronome in the city. A lot of people from school should be there. It'll be cool. Come with me."

"Nah. Look, Spoon, I'm just gonna chill and have myself a little drink and go to sleep."

"Donavin, I'm going to be at your house in two hours. I recommend that you be dressed." Spoon hung up the phone without waiting for a reply.

Spoon arrived as he said he would and Donavin was dressed and ready to go as requested.

The party at Metronome was live. Donavin went straight to the bar and ordered two Thug Passions. He and Spoon sat back checking out the ladies until they were spotted by a few members of their favorite fraternity. Some of the guys they had fought with at the Ball were also home for the holidays. Richard Smithers and company wasted no time in approaching them.

"Donavin." Smithers greeted him and extended his hand.

Donavin responded by glancing down at Smithers' hand before turning away.

Smithers whispered to one of his boys behind him and said, "Look at his eyes. Billion Dollar Alcoholic." His friend began to laugh.

"Do you need an instant replay of Homecoming, asshole?" Donavin asked, as he tilted his head to the side.

"Jasmine's a lovely girl," Smithers said to his boys but loud enough for Donavin to hear. "She was at Justin's with us a little while ago. I'm mad at her, though. I hardly get to see my boy, Allen, and she goes and steals him away from us. I mean, I guess they decided to go off and do their own thing." Smithers shrugged his shoulders as his frat brothers laughed.

Donavin was not at all pleased to hear that Allen and Jasmine had gone off somewhere together. He was ready to go at it again. However, he decided to play it cool instead of giving Smithers the reaction that he wanted. He cracked a smile and whispered in Smithers ear, "You're not going to know when it's coming, or even that I'm the one that did it to you. But I'm going to make sure that you get yours and there will be absolutely nothing that you can do about it."

Donavin finished both of his drinks with two large gulps, then turned and walked away. Spoon stared at the Betas momentarily and said, "Punk asses," before he followed Donavin.

One of the Betas said something back, but not loud enough for it to easily be heard. Spoon turned around quickly and asked, "What the fuck did you say?"

The miscellaneous Beta flinched when Spoon challenged him. "I thought as much," Spoon said and strode away.

Donavin and Spoon then got a table, and Donavin called the waitress over so he could order more drinks.

"Don't you think you should slow down?" Spoon cautioned.

"Look, man, you asked me to come out with you to the club. Why are you giving me static about having a few drinks?"

"D, I just watched you down two Thug Passions like they were nothing. I can see it in your face that you've been drinking all day. I'm just a little concerned about you is all."

"Don't be, Spoon." The waitress arrived and Donavin ordered two more Thug Passions.

It wasn't long before they began to attract a female audience. For the rest of the night, they chilled at the table while various women sat down as if they were being interviewed for the job of being one of their girls.

At about four A.M., they left the club with their pockets full of phone numbers. They stumbled to Spoon's Porsche, which was parked in a pay parking lot on Twenty-second Street between Broadway and Sixth Avenue.

"On to Jersey."

"Nah, man," Donavin was drunk and leaning to the side. "Just drop me at Twentieth and Broadway."

"Are you sure, D? Where are you going?"

"It's cool, I've just got some business to take care of is all."

"Donavin, I can't in good conscience just drop you off in the middle of the city like this, especially not in your condition. Just tell me where you want to go and I'll give you a lift."

"Look," Donavin slurred, "I don't need a baby sitter. You ain't my momma. Remember, she's dead."

They came to the corner of Twentieth and Broadway and Spoon reluctantly brought the car to a halt.

"All right. If you feel like being Atlanta brave, do what you must. Call me tomorrow and let me know you're all right."

"Aight," said Donavin as he fell out of the passenger door.

Spoon drove around the corner, but then turned around and pulled up behind Donavin. He was close enough to see him, but far away enough not be noticed. Donavin threw his arm up to hail a cab. Puzzled over his friend's actions, Spoon decided to follow him to see what was going on.

The ride took them over the Brooklyn Bridge and into Brooklyn Heights. Spoon wondered why the hell Donavin was going to Brooklyn so late. The cab pulled up at a brownstone and Donavin exited. Spoon watched Donavin ring the doorbell, then sit down on the steps when there was no answer. He rocked back and forth in the bitter cold with his face twisted. Spoon sat in his car watching for about thirty minutes and began to fall asleep. He awoke about two hours later at sunrise to find Donavin still waiting on the steps, rocking back and forth with greater force. But it looked like his rage was enough to keep him warm.

What the hell is he waiting on?

Then Spoon saw the reason Donavin was out there in the cold like a lunatic come strutting down the block. He sat up in his seat because it was about to be showtime.

"Donavin?" Jasmine looked very surprised to see him waiting on her stoop.

"Where the fuck are you coming from?" he asked through clenched teeth.

"Excuse me, but I think that you need to watch your tone. For your information I spent the night at a friend's house."

"Don't fucking stand here and treat me like I'm stupid. Why would I ask you if I didn't already know? Let me help you tell the truth. You spent the night with that muthafucka, Allen Pearson!"

Jasmine moved closer to him and smelled the alcohol on his breath. "Donavin, you're drunk. I'm not having this conversation with you while you're like this. And furthermore, to take a page out of your book, you're not my man, so don't worry about it."

Donavin was now pointing his index finger at her. "You know, I hope you and bitch ass Allen are very happy together. Stay the fuck out my life!"

He stomped off down the block and Jasmine ran into her apartment, visibly distressed over the exchange. Spoon saw his friend trying to hail a cab and drove up beside him.

Spoon beeped his horn to get Donavin's attention. "D, let me give you a ride, sir," Spoon offered.

"I'm cool," Donavin said, increasing his pace without looking in Spoon's direction.

Spoon's tires screeched as he sped up, then came to a sudden stop. He jumped out of the car, grabbed Donavin by the arm, and insisted that he get in the car. Donavin did so without a fight and soon they were on their way to New Jersey.

"I see Jasmine came in a little late," Spoon began.

"Whatever." Donavin acted like he didn't care. "She's a trick just like all the rest."

"Did you ask her what happened or did you just rant and rave?"

"I didn't have to rant and rave, Spoon. I already knew what happened."

"So that's it? You're not even going to hear her out? Even I, not being the nicest guy in the world, would give her the chance to explain herself. Or at least get that good break-up sex." Spoon chuckled.

Donavin laughed at Spoon's last comment, then got serious again. "Fuck it. I'm done. I'm going back to my old ways of just sexin' these girls and going on about my business. I've wasted a whole semester dealing with this bullshit. Whenever you try to act halfway decent with one of these females, they act dumb as hell."

"I couldn't agree more. I find that the only way to keep a woman in line is to treat her like shit. You don't understand how intellectually perplexing this is to me. Why do women, especially our sisters, not respect us unless we disrespect and disregard them?"

Donavin was glad that his friend understood him. "Every female that I have dogged out and treated like a ho has wanted to fucking marry me and pop out ten of my babies. I finally treat one like she's special and she's sluttin' around behind my back with Allen fucking Pearson. This shit makes no sense at all to me."

Spoon nodded his head. "I'm telling you, D. The better you treat them, the worse they act."

Jasmine lay across her bed sobbing. Even though she felt that Donavin had no right to verbally attack her that way, she knew that he wasn't quite himself as of late. She realized he was fighting inner demons and not winning the battle. She wanted so desperately to be there for him, but she knew that until he could come to grips with his mother's passing, she couldn't do anything for him.

Jasmine picked herself up and went back into the living room.

She sat in front of her stereo and popped her Alicia Keys CD into the CD player. She advanced to track number four and the song "Fallin'" began to play. The song, about someone who keeps falling in and out of love with a person who gives them both boundless pleasure and pain, felt like her theme music. As the song played, Jasmine's head began to pound. She pressed repeat and listened to the song over and over again.

How can I love someone who is such a player? Why doesn't he show me the attention and sensitivity he showed when we first met? Why didn't he look to me for stability and love in his time of need? Why doesn't he realize that I love him?

When she could no longer take being alone with her thoughts, she called Stacia.

"Hello," Stacia said groggily.

"Stacia," Jasmine said through her tears.

"What's wrong, sweetie?" Stacia awoke instantly and sat up in her bed.

"Donavin was waiting on my steps when I got in this morning. He knew I was with Allen last night."

Stacia groaned loudly. "He was trippin', huh?"

"We didn't even do anything, but he wouldn't let me explain. He had been drinking and just jumped down my throat. Then I kinda told him that he wasn't my man." Jasmine winced, hearing the words come from her mouth once again.

"I know he didn't like that. What did he say?"

"I don't know. I just remember the cursing," Jasmine replied. "Do you think I should call him and try to straighten things out?"

"Hell no!" Stacia protested. "You were exactly right. He isn't your man and you don't owe him an explanation for anything. You're a grown damn woman. Plus, once you start backing down, with brothers especially, they'll walk all over you. In Donavin's case, he's just going through a lot right now. It's not your fault. He's just choosing to take his frustrations out on you. You can't be his psychologist and his woman. He needs time to deal with his issues. Then maybe you can talk some sense into him."

"So, you think that I should just give him some space?"

"Shoot!" Stacia sucked her teeth. "If some fool who wasn't my man was at my door uninvited at the break of dawn waking up my neighbors, I'd cut his ass loose with the quickness. If I were you, I would give him time to get his act together."

"You're right, Stacia," Jasmine said, covering her eyes with her hand.

"Jas, don't get so upset. He'll calm down. If he doesn't, forget him. It's definitely his loss. Whatever you do, don't go calling and pouring your heart out. That's what they expect us to do, and when you do it they lose all respect."

After they'd hung up moments later, Jasmine was able to think a bit more clearly about everything that had happened. She'd given a great deal of emotional capital to Donavin and didn't want things to end up the way they were. However, she knew that Donavin was lost, and she felt that there was nothing she could do to help him find his way. Jasmine resolved to leave him alone until he was ready to talk to her. If their last conversation was any indication of future events, though, his coming to her was highly unlikely.

CHAPTER
TWENTY-TWO

January brought with it time to go back to school. Donavin headed to the airport without so much as a word to his father. Both had chosen silence as a way of dealing with their pain. Despite the beginning of a new year, he felt anything but refreshed. He appeared as if he was punishing himself for some dastardly wrong. He had lost about fifteen pounds, and his appetite for alcohol and self-destruction were looming larger. Instead of going to class he wasted most days watching television and staring blankly into space.

For the next four months, the BDP Penthouse had become Donavin's self-imposed jail cell. During this period, he made no attempts to reconcile with God or Jasmine and basically ignored his father. He only ventured forth from their apartment for an occasional class, food and, of course, more liquor.

His friends often struggled with him to snap out of the funk that he was in, but he would have no part of it. One April evening they suggested a Boys Night In and Donavin reluctantly agreed. Spoon and J.R. returned home to find the house dark and quiet. Spoon flicked on the lights while J.R. went to retrieve Donavin.

"Hey, dawg. You in dere? We got hot wings and *Shaft* on DVD. Samuel L. Jackson is so fuckin' hard." J.R. knocked at Donavin's door. "Donavin," he grunted again. "Answer me when I'm talkin' to you, bruh."

J.R. huffed and entered the room, but no Donavin. He saw that the bathroom door was closed, so he called to him once more. "Donavin, you ain't shittin', is you?"

There was still no response. J.R. sniffed under the door to avoid any surprises, then decided to enter the bathroom. He walked in to see Donavin lying facedown on the floor with an empty bottle of vodka at his side.

"Spoon!" J.R. called out with fear. "Spoon, git yo' high yella ass in here, dawg!"

Spoon dropped his chicken wing and sprang to his feet. He was at J.R's side in a couple of seconds.

"Oh shit! Wake up, D!" Spoon rolled Donavin onto his back and slapped him in the face. Donavin's head rolled around like it was on a swivel and he mumbled something unintelligible. Once they caught a whiff of his breath, they knew that he wasn't dead but merely drunk out of his mind.

"I know what to do," J.R. said, smirking. He began to run some cold water in the tub and filled it up about halfway.

"You're not about to do what I think you are?" Spoon asked as he smirked back.

"Yep, dat fool 'bout to go bobbin' fuh apples, but ain't gon' be no apples."

With that, J.R. picked Donavin up and began dunking his head into the ice cold water over and over again. When the cold water began to hit him in the face, Donavin began to resist.

"Git dis fool's legs." J.R. enlisted Spoon's help.

Spoon did so and made Donavin helpless against J.R.'s dunking attack.

"You wanna drink like a fish den enjoy dis water, fool."

Donavin gasped for air and flailed in the water, trying to talk and fight back.

At this point in the assault, Donavin was halfway sober, which was as sober as he'd been in the last few months. Figuring that they had proven their point, Spoon and J.R let him up.

Donavin sat on the bathroom floor, soaking wet and clutching his knees.

"What da fuck is da matta wit' you? Dawg, I know you miss yo' momma, but you gots to move on. She wit' God now, bruh!" J.R. shouted at Donavin.

"Yeah, D, you've got so many things going for you. This isn't you." Spoon picked up the bottle and tossed it in the trash.

"What the fuck do you guys know about it?" Donavin looked up at Spoon and J.R. "I'm sick and tired of you guys preaching all the damn time."

Spoon took umbrage to Donavin's comment and snatched him up from the floor.

"Look at yourself." Spoon gripped Donavin by the back of his neck and forced him to face the mirror. "This has gone too far. I know you miss your mom, but she wouldn't want to see you living like this."

"Yo' ass need to take a break on all dat drankin'."

Donavin had a moment of clarity. He looked at the reflection in the mirror and didn't see the person he knew he was. He didn't like who he had allowed himself to become.

"Damn." Donavin groaned and placed his hands over his face to block the sight of his own image. "This isn't fair, y'all." Tears began to stream down his face.

"Nothing ever is." Spoon put his arms around Donavin's shoulder.

"Everythang is gon' be okay, D. We yo' family too, dawg. You know we got yo' back straight up and down."

"I know," Donavin said, wiping his eyes and turning toward his friends. "I feel like shit. I can't keep doing this."

"Sounds like the real D is coming back, J.R." Spoon grinned.

Donavin smiled as well. "Thanks fellas. I love y'all."

"He's thankin' us fuh whoopin' his ignant ass?" J.R. joked. "No problem. We can start beatin' up on ya every time you start actin' crazy."

"My friend, we're going to let you detox now. Come on, Big Country, it's getting late. Let's go start this movie." Spoon led the way out of Donavin's room.

"Dawg, I know what da time is. Don't let me have to go Tony Montana on yo' pretty muthafuckin' ass."

"Go ahead, J.R. I'm just gonna get in some dry clothes and go to sleep. I'll holla at y'all in the morning."

"All right, playa. You gon' be all right, dawg."

"I know, man. I know."

Donavin dried out for the rest of the night and decided that it was time for him to get his life back on track. It was time to live up to his words at Thanksgiving dinner. It was time for him to start spending the rest of his days proving his love in his mother's memory. He picked up the phone shortly after waking up and called his father.

"Pop."

"Son, it's so good to hear your voice. I've missed you."

"Me too. I've been having a tough time with everything that's been going on. I just want you to know that I love you, and I do want you to be a part of my life."

"Donavin, you don't know how much it means to me to hear you say that. I know I should have been there for you through all of this. It's just that I lost my best friend of twenty-five years."

"Yeah, I know."

"Your mom was the compassionate one who nurtured you. I've always been the disciplinarian in the house. I saw my job as basically bailing you out when you got into jams and slapping your tail when you needed it. This tough guy shit of being silent and not helping each other out during this time was stupid."

"I agree, Dad. I know."

"It's hard for me to be alone, Donavin. The last time I was alone, I was younger than you. I was the original Mack Daddy."

Donavin laughed at his father's usage of slang.

"Son, there's a bond between a mother and her son that is indescribable and irreplaceable. I know you miss your mom. I miss my wife, too."

"I understand, Pop. We just have to carry on the best we can without her."

"Donavin, if you need anything, or you just want to talk, please know that I am here for you twenty-four seven, as you kids say."

"Thanks, Pop. As a matter of fact, I could use some help on my presidential speech for graduation. I've been a little out of it lately and I haven't got a clue about what I'm going to say. I know you're great at this kind of thing, Congressman Jackson."

"Donavin, I could come up with some really good things for you to say, but I'm sure that with some thought you can come up with great things. I can, however, provide some inspiration."

"Inspiration?"

"Yeah, inspiration. Like a four-day weekend in Jamaica. Why don't you, Adam, and J.R. head down there and take a few days to relax and unwind on me?"

"I can't. I've got to write this speech and study for my exams."

"Boy, life is too short. Schoolwork has never been hard for you and sometimes you need to take a vacation to get your head together. As a matter of fact, I insist on it. You guys will have the tickets tomorrow."

"If you insist, Pop."

The two men continued to catch up with one another and reaffirm their bond. Donavin now had something to look forward to.

"Simon and Rothstein, Jasmine DeRoche speaking."

"Hello, Simon and Rothstein Jasmine DeRoche speaking," the distinguished voice on the other end said.

Jasmine paused and raised her eyebrows. She recognized the line, but she was slower to recognize the voice. "Who is calling please?" Jasmine asked sternly.

"This is Donavin Jackson, Senior."

"Oh hi, Mr. Jackson," Jasmine said warmly. "How are you?"

"I'm well and yourself, sweetheart?"

"Oh, I'm . . . okay, I guess."

"Well, I've got an offer that will make you feel better than okay. How would you like to go to Jamaica for four days?"

"That's mighty tempting, but if we ran away to Jamaica together, what would people say? That may hurt your political career," Jasmine joked.

He chuckled. "Listen, I'm sending Donavin, J.R., and Adam. I want you, Stacia, and Carmen to join them. My treat. What do you say?"

"That's very nice, but me and Donavin are kinda on the outs. I'm pretty sure he wouldn't want to be on a vacation with me, of all people."

"I think he does. He just hasn't had the words to tell you himself."

"I'm sorry, Mr. Jackson, but I have to decline the invitation."

"How about this then? Jamaica is a nice size island. If you guys don't hit it off, then just stay away from each other. I've seen you two together, and I see my wife and myself twenty-five years ago.

Life's too short to let opportunity slip through one's fingers."

Jasmine thought for a moment and then caved in. She wanted to go on a vacation and a free one was just what the doctor ordered. Jasmine also wanted to see if what she once had with Donavin could still be salvaged.

"Okay."

"Okay, you'll go?"

"Yes, sir."

"Beautiful! Do you think your friends can make it, too?"

"For a free trip to Jamaica? Those two will be on the plane, believe me."

"The tickets will be there tomorrow, my dear."

CHAPTER
TWENTY-THREE

Donavin and company boarded the plane for their trip to the isle of Jamaica early Thursday morning. They were all excited at the prospect of getting away from Atlanta and basking in the island sun for a few days. They arrived at Donald Sangster International Airport in Montego Bay and were taken by shuttle to their resort in Negril.

"Man, deez Jamaican breezies gon' love me down here," J.R. said, rubbing himself down with tanning lotion.

"Pass me that." Donavin motioned to J.R. "The sun is gonna be hell on your beige behind, huh, Spoon?" Donavin teased Spoon as he liberally applied sunblock to his shoulders and chest.

"Just makes me golden brown, D. You better watch out. I'm about to invade your territory," Spoon quipped in stride as he eyed himself in the mirror.

"Dawg, finish up and git yo' house slave-lookin' ass ready."

They all grabbed their backpacks and headed to the pool area of the resort. Though the temperature was hot, a gentle breeze came off the Caribbean Sea. The cloudless blue sky combined with the light crashing of the surf made the day a gorgeous ten. They approached the pool and found nothing but beautiful young people soaking up the golden rays of the sun.

"Got dang! I love yo' daddy so much right now, D!" J.R. was definitely feeling the vibe.

"And how," Spoon concurred.

They soaked in the scenery for a couple of minutes and then something caught Donavin's eye. He noticed a woman with a caramel complexion and long braided hair wearing sunglasses, a floral bikini, and a straw hat lying on a beach chair across the pool. He didn't say a word to Spoon or J.R. as he moved to take a closer look, then suddenly turned and headed for the hotel lobby.

"Where dat fool goin'?" J.R. asked testily.

Spoon shrugged and then looked across the pool. "Oh shit!" Spoon exclaimed. "That's Jasmine, Stacia, and Carmen over there."

"Git da fuck outta here, dawg. Don't be playin' wit my emotions."

"Look for yourself!"

J.R. looked in the direction Spoon pointed. "Ay papi!" J.R. mocked Carmen's accent. "Even dough dis goes against my sand to da beach policy, I'm gon' wear dat ass out one mo' gen!"

"I'm guessing that's why Mr. Jackson is cowering in the lobby right now."

"Please go git dat fool so we can beat deez broads. He bein' straight up silly right now."

Spoon walked into the lobby and found Donavin standing behind a pillar.

"What's up, D?" he asked casually.

"Nothing, man. Just chillin'."

"Let's skip the small talk. I take it that you're standing here because you saw a certain group of young ladies across the pool."

"You're a genius, Spoon." Donavin was sarcastic.

"I'm glad you've finally realized it. Far too often it goes unrecognized. But anyway, why are we standing here talking to each other while those girls are here at the same hotel, at the same time, obviously to see us? Does that really make any kind of sense to you, Donavin?"

"Dammit, I know my Pop bought their tickets. I'm going to chat with him when I get home."

"Well, in the meantime, stop being a big baby and come on."

"Nah, I say we post up at a table near the pool and wait until they notice us. Power positioning, my friend. I'm sure you're familiar."

"You're learning, young Donavin." Spoon smiled. "I'll grab J.R."

Spoon strolled back over to J.R. and tried to get him to walk over to the secluded table that Donavin selected. At that moment Carmen rolled onto her stomach, exposing her thong. J.R.'s mouth flung wide open and Spoon followed suit.

"The Lord is definitely good. Come on. Let's go sit down over there with Donavin and let them come to us," Spoon said as he tried to nudge J.R. away.

At first J.R. refused and said, "Jus' give me one mo' minute, dawg." He looked at Carmen's rear end for a second more and said, "Betta make dat an hour."

Spoon then grabbed him and physically ushered him toward the table. The men sat together and watched as the girls sunbathed until dusk. Spoon and J.R. had enough rum to make the most hardcore drinker pass out. Donavin decided to abstain and just drink fruit juice.

The smell of the ocean and the sound of reggae music created an environment of total relaxation and leisure. It seemed like all the problems of the world were a million miles away as they watched the miracle of the Jamaican sunset.

"You guys stood by me when my mother passed. I love you bruthas. That's my word."

Spoon shook his head. "D, you don't even have to say it.

We know."

"Somebody gots to look out fuh yo' punk ass when you wanna start fightin' ten dudes at once. We da only fools crazy enough to be down fuh yo' ass like dat."

They all enjoyed a boisterous laugh and raised their drinks to toast.

"To good friends," Spoon announced.

Donavin added, "To good times."

"To hearty ass beats!" J.R. gulped his drink down and slammed the glass on the table.

"Amen to that, papi," an accented voice concurred.

The BDP had stopped paying attention to what was going on poolside, and the girls had snuck up on them. The party was crashed. Donavin only saw Stacia and Carmen. He didn't see Jasmine, but he knew that she was close to him. Donavin stood and turned around to see her. He took a deep breath and reached his arms out. They embraced and it felt as it had when they held each other for the first time. Time had healed old wounds.

"Dat's what I like to see," said J.R., wrapping his arms around Carmen as well.

"He's not going anywhere, mami. He won't turn into a pumpkin if you let him go," added Carmen.

Jasmine continued to hold Donavin for a few seconds more. The sun had now disappeared over the horizon and there was an air of calm and closeness as the three couples ordered dinner at the poolside restaurant. They feasted on lobster, jerk chicken, curried shrimp, rice and peas, and plantains. As each couple satisfied their appetites, they broke away relatively quickly with no explanations until Donavin and Jasmine were left alone.

"Is this déjà vu or what?" Jasmine said.

"For real." Donavin smiled at her.

"Your father is the sweetest man in the world. I was so nervous about how you would be toward me. I'm glad I came."

"I'm glad you're here, too. I do, however, have one question for you."

Jasmine's heart sank into the pit of her stomach because the smile that Donavin had displayed before was replaced by a more serious expression.

"Did you sleep with Allen Pearson that night?"

Jasmine breathed a sigh of relief and answered, "No, I didn't. Actually, Stacia and I hung out with him and some of his friends. It was late and we were closer to Stacia's spot. I spent the night at her place and came home to see this ranting, drunk, crazy man in front of my apartment. Now that that's all cleared up, did you ever sleep with Angela?"

Donavin cringed at the mention of Angela's name. "Let's get in the hot tub," Donavin returned without answering the question.

"Yeah . . . okay," Jasmine said, pursing her lips.

They walked by the pool and stepped into the hot tub. Jasmine leaned against Donavin with her back to him. It felt heavenly as he held her in his arms.

"What do you think our friends are doing now?" Donavin rekindled the conversation.

"Gettin' a hearty ass beat!" Jasmine imitated J.R.

They laughed together.

Jasmine turned around to face Donavin. "So, does my question not deserve to be answered?"

Donavin sighed and looked into her eyes. He held her hands under the water. "Look, Jas, I won't lie and say I didn't think about it. I called her one night to come over and—"

Jasmine tried to hide the hurt she felt, but it was written all over her face. "I don't think I want to hear any more, Donavin." She quietly cut him off.

"I think you do. Her roommate answered and lied about where

she was. I got suspicious and decided to be nosey. So I went over to her apartment to see what was really going on and saw her outside with Jamal Davis from the Hawks. I had seen enough when she started to give dude a blowjob in the parking lot. I never really talked to her after that. That whole incident was kind of a turn-off."

Jasmine began to laugh hysterically. Donavin began to chuckle with her. "And what's so funny?"

"How could you ever talk to a ho like that?" She wrapped her arms around him. "I'm just glad that you didn't do anything with her. I heard that she's fast with cats with money. After a night with her, it might not be a bad idea to get tested."

The lanterns next to the hot tub flickered, and a cool island breeze came upon them. Donavin looked into Jasmine's eyes and said for the first time to any woman besides his mother, "I love you."

"I love you, too, Brown Eyes." She then gently pressed her lips against his and straddled him in the water. "I'm going to do something that's against my better judgement." She threw her braids to the side. "I'm going to let you be my man and let you treat me like your lady. You will be attentive, sensitive, honest, and, most of all, faithful. What do you think about that, Billion Dollar Playboy?"

Donavin fought the instinct to continue the life of being the player and the ladies' man. He resisted because something deep inside told him that this was the time and she was the one.

"I think that I can work with that," he replied.

"You think? I need you to know, Brown Eyes."

"I do, Baby Girl."

They kissed again and held each other close. Donavin then began to remove Jasmine's bikini top.

Jasmine pulled back and sucked her teeth. "Not so fast, my brother. That's not what this relationship is going to be based on."

"What are you talking about? We've already done this part

before. I haven't had any in months. Come on now, I got needs."

"You're my man now. You're not cut off completely, but you do have to accummulate a certain number of cool points before I give you some again."

"I don't know about all that." Donavin poked out his lip with comical resentment. "That seems like a lot of work. I'm not used to all that."

Jasmine cocked her neck to the side and drew back. "Are you saying that I'm not worth the wait?"

"That about sums it up," he said, laughing.

Jasmine grabbed Donavin in a headlock. "Take it back!"

He complied and they embraced once again.

"Jas, I want nothing more than to show you how much I love you."

They talked for hours beside the hot tub until the morning sun arose. Donavin took a deep breath and blew it out as if releasing all the bad things that were bottled up inside of him. His thoughts then shifted to his mother and how he wished that she were still alive. That morning, as the sun rose in the east, he finally made his peace with her passing.

The next three days were partly fantasy and partly too wonderful for words. They rented scooters and traveled all over the island. Jasmine and Donavin always managed to sneak away and have their private time to connect. With each passing day, they fell deeper in love, and more importantly, deeper in respect.

On their last day in Jamaica, they took a ride to Dunn's River Falls in Ocho Rios. They climbed the falls, as is the custom, and Donavin felt inspired when he reached the top. He looked out over the cliffs and a moment later took a pen and paper from his backpack.

"I've gotta write this speech now," he said.

Everyone just kind of nodded as he went to be alone behind a small hill on the other side of the waterfall. About two hours later he returned to the group with a finished presidential speech in hand.

The weekend soon ended and the time came for them to head home—the women to New York, and the men to Atlanta. They gathered at the airport terminal.

"I know y'all comin' to watch me—I mean us—graduate next week, right?" J.R. asked the girls.

"Hell yeah," Carmen promised before anyone else could answer.

"I'll be there," Stacia answered. "Gotta see my sorors walk."

"I wouldn't miss it." Jasmine kissed Donavin on the lips.

"Anybody got a barf bag?" J.R. joked.

"Air Jamaica flight forty to Atlanta now boarding at gate five." The boarding announcement blared over the loudspeaker.

"That's us, gentlemen. Let's do it," Spoon said. He walked over to Stacia and whispered, "If you need a place to stay when you come down for graduation, you've got my number." She smiled at him, he kissed her temple, then boarded the plane after saying his goodbyes to Carmen and Jasmine.

By this time, J.R. was putting the same bug in Carmen's ear. "Girrrrrrl," he whispered. He must have said something very pleasing to her because a devilish grin formed on her face and then she broke into laughter. He said goodbye and went to find his seat on the plane.

"I'd better be going, too," Donavin said to Jasmine.

"Next week, Brown Eyes."

After one last kiss, Donavin went to join his friends for their journey back to the states.

CHAPTER TWENTY-FOUR

"I can't believe we're about to be alums tomorrow," Spoon remarked from his seat on the living room couch opposite Donavin and J.R.

"I know," Donavin said, "but it ain't over yet, at least for some people. We've got a little unfinished business to take care of."

"I love it when you be talkin' deviously." J.R leaned forward in his seat.

Donavin got on the phone and asked Winston Charles to come over. The doorbell rang ten minutes later.

"What's going on, man?" Winston blew in with a whirlwind of enthusiasm, all too anxious to see what the BDP were up to. "What's up, guys?"

"You know we've had several run-ins with the Betas in the past," Donavin began.

"Yeah, man, I don't like any of those guys. I know you must wanna get some revenge before you graduate. If you do, I wanna help." Donavin, Spoon, and J.R. all smiled as Winston played right into their plan.

"Listen, Winston, I think Richard Smithers needs to disappear for a little while."

"Like kidnapping? No doubt, we can keep him at my uncle's house out in Lawrenceville." Winston was actually serious, which made them all a little bit nervous.

"Uh . . . nah . . . nothing like that, Winston. But you're a real whiz when it comes to computers. I'm talking about making him disappear from the university's student records. Something like losing his tuition payments or last semester's courses. Something to that effect."

Winston seemed to think that this idea was somehow riskier than locking Smithers in his uncle's basement. "I don't know, Donavin. That's a protected mainframe. If I get caught, I could get into a lot of trouble. But I might be able to write a special program—"

"Of course you can, Winston. That's the spirit," Donavin encouraged. "Can you do it today?"

"I'll have to use my own equipment." Winston was apprehensive again. "This is really illegal, guys. I don't know."

"I'm sorry, Winston." Donavin adopted a comforting tone. "What can the BDP do for you? It would be unfair of us to ask such a large favor for nothing in return."

Winston looked down at the ground. "Well, there is one thing. How about . . . honorary BDP membership?"

"Dawg, you straight up shits creek wit'out a paddle on dat request, bruh."

"Now wait a minute," Spoon said, determined to come to an agreeable end. "We are asking the man to break some fairly serious computer laws. Winston, we honorarily welcome you into the Billion Dollar Playboys."

"Spoon!" Interrupted J.R. in disagreement.

Spoon reasoned. "I think that watching Smithers being yanked from that graduation line tomorrow morning is more than an even trade-off for a BDP membership."

Grins lit up the room at Spoon's explanation of the situation.

"Dat would be da all time biggest payback of paybacks." J.R. started sliding across the floor like James Brown. "I'm wit' it." He gave his approval.

"I won't let you guys down," Winston said as he ran out the door to his car.

"Hello." Donavin turned off the vacuum cleaner.

"Hey, Brown Eyes, what are you up to?" Jasmine mumbled dejectedly into the receiver.

"Just straightening up a little. What's wrong, girl? I haven't done anything since I've been back. If somebody told you I did, they're lying."

"I can't believe this is happening to me," she said sadly.

"Jas, you're scaring me. I don't think I can take much more drama this year."

"Oh, it's nothing for you to get upset about. I just got put on this deal, and I'll be stuck in the office all weekend. I have to miss your graduation, sweetie."

"Oh," he said quietly. "Well . . . it's not your fault. Things like this happen. I'll see you when I get back home."

"I'm so sorry. I would really get out of it if I could, but I can't."

"It's cool, Baby Girl. I'll see you in a few weeks." Donavin was hurt that she wouldn't be there but did his best to hide his disappointment.

"I'll call you in the morning before you go to the ceremony. Okay, Brown Eyes? I love you."

"I love you, too."

Donavin hung up the phone and then gazed out of the window. He was saddened by the fact that neither his mother nor Jasmine would be attending his graduation. Just as he felt himself falling into a funk the phone rang again.

"Donavin, mission accomplished. Smithers has been erased."

Donavin's face spread into a wide smile. "Best news I've heard all day, Winston. Old Smithers is not going to be a happy camper when his narrow ass gets the boot from the line mañana. Was it difficult?"

"Not really," Winston said smugly. "The university's mainframe has a childish encryption code that was like cracking open a piggy bank. How pathetic."

"Glad to hear it. You've performed a valuable service for mankind. The BDP, of which you are an honorary member, commends you."

Winston had never received such accolades from Donavin and scooped it up with the biggest spoon in town. "I'll be cheering for you guys at the ceremony."

"Thanks, chief. Oh yeah, I need you to do me another favor tomorrow. Nothing big, I promise. I'll call you in the morning."

"Okay?" Winston replied, apprehension evident in his voice.

Later that night, as Donavin gazed up at the stars and pondered the events of the past year, a sense of calm came over him. Serenity filled his heart from having made peace with his life and being finally able to look forward to the future without being weighed down by emotional baggage of the past.

CHAPTER TWENTY-FIVE

Graduation Day brought a sea of people to the Stratford University campus. Black college graduations were always special events because everyone in the family attends. Parents, sisters, brothers, the father's uncle's cousin's momma—every damn body shows up.

Spoon rigged it so that the BDP would all walk together at the head of the line, and then have their names announced together at the end of the ceremony. Saving the best for last was the planned theme.

All of the graduates assembled in the Quad before the traditional walk over the hill to the campus green for the commencement exercises. The graduates were forming their processional line in alphabetical order when everyone's attention was suddenly captured by a ruckus toward the end of the line.

"Well, young man," Dean Tilden explained to Smithers, "your name isn't on the list, so you must step out of line."

"What? What do you mean my name isn't on the list?" Smithers asked frantically.

With Spoon and J.R. walking alongside him, Donavin went to see what the problem was. "Whatever could be the problem on this glorious graduation day?"

A voice behind Smithers said, "That man's name ain't on the list. I'd be mad as hell if they tried to kick my black ass out this line."

Smithers' face burned with exasperation. He hated the fact that Donavin was watching his world crash around him.

Donavin walked over to Smithers and whispered, "It's truly unfortunate that something like this has to happen, your family being here to see you graduate and all. You must have enemies in high places." Donavin winked, smiled, then walked away.

"Fuck you," Smithers screamed at Donavin's back. He broke from line to rush Donavin, but he was restrained by some of the other students.

"Whoa, whoa, Gary Coleman. It looks like you're the one who's fucked. It's not *my* fault that you're not graduating today," Donavin said sarcastically. "There's always summer school, partna."

The BDP and the graduates within earshot laughed. Smithers ran from the line fuming with humiliation and the knowledge that Donavin had had the last laugh.

The walk over the hill to the campus green was majestic. It felt as if they were headed to another place, to uncharted territory, not just over to the campus lawn where they had all walked thousands of times before. The audience of almost ten thousand was fully assembled as "Pomp and Circumstance" blared over the loudspeakers. The BDP led the class and as they descended the hill thousands of flashbulbs went off. The day had finally arrived. Four years of hard work, trials, and tribulations had led them all to this point.

As they were about to take their seats, Donavin noticed his father out of the corner of his eye sitting in the first row. He was impeccably dressed in a navy blue Armani suit, and he glowed with pride at the sight of his son. They made eye contact momentarily and waved, then Donavin took his seat along with the rest of the graduating class.

The ceremony began with President Walter Massley welcoming all of the family, friends, faculty, and students who had come to share in the joyous occasion. The commencement wasn't anything eventful with its seemingly endless schedule of rehearsed monologues and boring speeches.

Donavin grew anxious as his time drew nearer. He hadn't really practiced the speech that he had written in Jamaica and didn't know how it might be received. Afraid, he was not, for he knew that his mother was looking down on him and that he would draw from her the strength he needed. He slid into a slight daydream until he heard President Massley announce his name. The audience erupted with applause.

Donavin rose and approached the stage. Halfway there, he stopped and turned. He motioned to Spoon and J.R. to join him as he spoke. They were taken aback, but they were his friends and they had his back.

They walked over to him and Spoon whispered, "What's the deal, sir?"

Donavin responded simply, "I want you guys to join me. We've done everything else together these last four years. Besides, I could use some moral support. I also haven't rehearsed this speech, so I'm not quite sure what the hell I'm going to say."

"Jus' like a brutha," J.R. joked under his breath. "Jus' woefully unprepared."

Donavin climbed the stairs to the stage with his friends following closely behind him.

Carmen and Stacia were watching the BDP walk across the stage when a voice whispered, "What did I miss?"

"I thought you were working today?" Stacia said as she removed her purse from the seat beside her.

"I just got up early this morning and thought about what was more important to me. I see you saved me a seat," Jasmine responded.

"I knew you'd be here." Stacia winked and hugged her.

"Shh, chicas!" Carmen hushed them. "Donavin's about to give his speech."

Donavin looked out over the crowd and its mere size overwhelmed him for a moment. He clutched both sides of the podium for support, then glanced almost subconsciously at Spoon and J.R. standing a few feet behind him nodding reassuringly. He then looked down at the notes he had prepared in Jamaica, crinkled them up and threw them on the ground. The crowd gasped.

"Welcome, family, friends, faculty and students," he began. "I had some remarks written down, but I think I'm just going to speak from the heart to you all this morning, if it's all the same. I promise to be brief. First of all, I want to thank God for His blessings and for allowing all of us to be here together today." He shot a glance over his shoulder at J.R.

J.R. began to clap and the audience followed.

"As many of you may know and for those who don't, last semester I lost one of the most important people in my life, my mother." He felt a lump begin to rise in his throat and knew that he'd better continue before he got too choked up. "She was a Stratford alum, class of 1977. She was the woman who gave me life, took care of me when I was sick, listened to me, and loved me. When she took ill, my parents hid the truth from me in hopes that she would recover and get better. She never did. She held on just long enough to say goodbye to me. That night in the hospital when she passed, I couldn't believe how this woman who had once been so strong had become so weak. She had an inner strength and a compassion that touched everyone she met. I remember when I was five, we were going on vacation, just me, my mom, and my pop. I was afraid to fly and started freaking out on the plane. My pops got really annoyed and said, 'Boy, if you don't sit down and shut up, you'll be wearing three shoes. Two on your feet and one in your behind.'"

Laughter spread through the audience.

"I love you, Pop," Donavin nodded in his father's direction and continued with a smile. "But my mom was just so patient with me. She sat me next to her, lifted the divider between the two seats and stroked my head as I continued to cry in her lap. I don't really remember the rest of the flight or even the rest of trip. I just remember my mother quietly rubbing my head and making me feel at ease with something as simple as her touch. For years I took that for granted.

"Let me see a show of hands. How many of you have cut mom off on the phone in order to go hang out with your friends or do something else that wasn't that important?"

Very few hands went up among the graduates.

Donavin shook his head and said, "Since lying is a sin, I guess a whole bunch of y'all are going straight to hell." More laughter ensued and Donavin got almost one hundred percent participation.

"That's more like it. I know I did it all the time. I'm sure y'all know the lines: 'Sorry, mom, I'm mad tired. We'll hang another time.' 'I'll call you later, mom.' 'I'm on my way out the door, mom.'"

The graduates nodded their heads in agreement.

"And now I've run out of the time that I thought that I had endless amounts of. At the hospital, I held her hand at the very second her grip loosened and she slipped away. That woman held on through all the pain that the cancer caused her just to make sure that she was able to say goodbye to me. As my father says, there is an inexplicable bond between mother and child.

"I blamed God for a long time for taking her from me. I called Him every name that you could imagine. Whether you call him Jehovah, Allah, Buddah, or Yahweh, I hated all of them. How could He, who was supposed to be inherently good, just up and take my mother so early? I asked what I did to deserve that punishment."

"What I learned was that God took one thing, but left me with so many others. He left me with a father who loves me and who I love dearly and two of the best friends any man would be lucky to have. Let me not insult them by calling them friends." He looked over his shoulder at Spoon and J.R. and said, "These are my brothers. He also sent me a woman who is warm and loving and good." He paused as a tear rolled down his cheek. "What I'm trying to tell all of you is that you need to take the time to show the people you care about how much you love them each and every single day. I want all the graduates to rise."

They all did so.

"Now turn around," Donavin continued. "We're a small graduating class of nine hundred, yet we have almost ten thousand people here today. Ten thousand! Do you have any idea how powerful that is? People are here from all over the country, from all over the world. And you all can't call home to your families? Just to say 'hey mom, I don't want anything, I just called to see how you're doing.' Or to say 'mom, I love you.'"

Mothers throughout the crowd agreed wholeheartedly and cries of "amen" and "hallelujah" rang out.

"As I look over this class of 2002, I see bright, intelligent, successful, young black people. I see future lawyers, doctors, business leaders. Whatever you want to be! But none of that means a damn thing," he said, pounding his fist against the podium, "if the people you love aren't there to share it with you. Make sure the people you love know it every day."

He paused and looked up towards the heavens. "I love you. Those three words are so powerful. Like me, those people who were in the World Trade Center and the Pentagon don't have any more chances to tell the people they love how they feel about them. But most, if not all, of you do. You never know when the opportunity to say those words to someone may disappear. Best of luck, class of 2002. Be steadfast, be strong, be true. Do great things!"

"That's my baby!" With tears in her eyes, Jasmine stood up and raised her voice over the din of the crowd.

A thunderous ovation started. Donavin stepped away from the podium, blew a kiss up to heaven, then touched his heart and pointed to his father.

Donavin's words halted the program for twenty minutes because all of the graduates had taken what he said to heart and gone to find their families. The scene was an outpouring of love with entire families hugging and crying together. They realized how blessed they all were to be there together on a day that celebrated this spiritual rite of passage.

Mr. Jackson couldn't contain the joy he felt at hearing his son's words and rushed the stage to be with him. He joined his son, Spoon and J.R. in a teary-eyed group hug.

"Man," J.R. said, trying to compose himself. "I gotta go find my momma."

"Me, too." Spoon dried his eyes with a handkerchief.

Donavin was left alone embracing his father on stage.

"Your mother would have been so proud of you if she were here today," Mr. Jackson said to his son.

"She is here, Pop. I know she's watching," Donavin assured his father. He then looked up and saw a vision making her way through the crowd.

"Oh, Donavin!" Jasmine said, throwing her arms around him.

"Baby Girl, I thought you weren't going to make it today." Donavin hugged her tightly.

"I went with what was more important."

Donavin shook his head. "I had a premonition you'd be here."

"Hey, Miss Jasmine." Mr. Jackson greeted and embraced her.

"Hey," Donavin protested jokingly, "get your hands off my woman, Pop. This one's all mine."

President Massley stepped to the microphone, wiping his brow with his handkerchief. "That was some speech, folks. A lot of people needed to hear that. Let's have another hand for Student Government Association President Donavin Jackson."

The audience applauded once more. President Massley then spoke again. "Please, if everyone could please find their seats."

Things settled down and people started to amble back toward their seats. Donavin, Jasmine, and Mr. Jackson slowly filed off the stage.

"Jasmine," Donavin whispered softly in her ear, "go back to your seat, but stay close. There's something I need to ask you after the ceremony."

Mr. Jackson smiled to himself at seeing Donavin and Jasmine together. *Jamaica does the trick every time.*

President Massley announced the names of the graduating seniors. They were called one after the other until the last three came.

"Adam Christopher Witherspoon."

The crowd cheered loudly.

"Julian Roosevelt James."

"Julian Roosevelt?" the other graduates repeated. It was the first time most of them ever heard it.

J.R. stopped at the microphone on his way to get his diploma.

"Hey, y'all. Dat's all da jokes on my name I'm gon' have!"

He walked over to President Massley with a wide grin and gave him a bear hug, lifting him off the ground before he could give him his diploma. He then sauntered off the stage wearing his cowboy boots with a matching cowboy hat instead of the traditional mortarboard cap.

"Donavin Gregory Jackson, Junior."

Donavin received another standing ovation from the audience. He waved and took his stroll across the stage. President Massley handed him his diploma and said, "I'm so sorry for your loss. I know your mother is smiling down with pride at the man she raised." They embraced and Donavin rejoined J.R. and Spoon.

President Massley stepped closer to the podium wiping the sweat from his brow with his handkerchief and said, "I won't try to outdo the speech from earlier. Graduates of the class of 2002, please stand up. Please shift your tassels to the left. You have officially graduated from Stratford University."

The graduates threw their caps in the air and shouted with exuberance. Thousands of flashbulbs went off like it was a Hollywood premiere. "Pomp and Circumstance" came over the speakers once more and the graduates made their exit. Most of the audience left their seats to watch the graduates take their final walk together. The BDP brought up the rear of the line.

"Let's get closer so we can see them walking," Carmen urged Stacia and Jasmine.

They got close enough to see just as Angela was passing by. Jasmine scowled at her as if to threaten her with a repeat of their last encounter. Angela shifted her eyes and disappeared into the crowd. Then came the tail end of the line. Donavin noticed Jasmine and told Spoon and J.R. that he would catch up with them later.

Donavin walked up to her and kissed her on the forehead. "Baby Girl, take a walk with me."

The two walked hand in hand across the campus until they came to a bench surrounded by flowers, balloons, and ribbon in front of Gaines Hall.

"Have a seat." Donavin motioned for her to sit down and he sat beside her.

"Wow, they went all out for graduation this year," Jasmine said, admiring the decorations.

He smiled, caressing her hands in his. He made a mental note to thank Winston for decorating the bench.

"Jas, my mother lived here when she was in school."

Jasmine sighed. "Oh, Brown Eyes, although I only met your mother once, I could tell that she was a very special woman. She loved you so much."

"Yeah, she did. Pop proposed to my mom on this bench twenty-five years ago."

"Get outta here. That's so sweet. So this is where your parents got together, huh?"

"Yeah, that's why I brought you here." He sat closer to her and kissed her hand. He then looked toward heaven and took a deep breath, knelt in front of her on one knee and looked into her eyes. Jasmine's eyes widened and an expression of surprise formed on her face. "I love you, Jas. I want you to marry me."

Tears of joy, hope, and love began to stream down her face. She took Donavin in her arms and gently stroked the side of his head.

Does she say yes?

Be on the lookout for the sequel to

THAT'S THE WAY LOVE GOES

DISCUSSION QUESTIONS

1.   Donavin's initial attraction to Jasmine is on a physical level. When did it become deeper than that? At what point in the novel did they fall in love?

2.   Donavin and Jasmine have the quintessential love/hate relationship. Was this an accurate depiction of the struggles of young love?

3.   In an early conversation, Jasmine tells Donavin that she trusts him. However, her subsequent actions and words show a marked level of mistrust. Did she really trust Donavin?

4.   Donavin and his friends share a brotherly bond. How does Donavin differ from Spoon and J.R.? How is he the same?

5.   Jasmine bumped heads with Stacia at various points throughout the novel, but they still remained friends. Do you have friends that sometimes feel like enemies? If so, how do you deal with them, and do you feel that Jasmine dealt with Stacia realistically?

6.   *That's the Way Love Goes* is partially set on the campus of a fictional historically black university. Was the setting a realistic portrayal of black college life?

7.   This novel confronts the events of September 11th when Jasmine is potentially in harm's way. How did the events of that day affect the characters?

8.   Donavin had a very close relationship with his mother. Do you think that Donavin's parents should have kept his mother's illness a secret from him for as long as they did? Would Donavin have dealt with his mother's passing better if his father had allowed him to travel home upon hearing the news of her illness as opposed to at Thanksgiving when he only got to share her last moments?

9.   There is a spiritual element to the novel, but the characters didn't always follow the right path. How did their lifestyles clash with their faith?

10.   Were you surprised by the end of the novel? What was your reaction?

11.   How have the characters grown by the end of the novel?

12.   Can you identify with or do you know anyone like the characters in *That's the Way Love Goes?*

13.   If this novel were made into a movie, whom would you like to see cast in the roles?

14.   There is a sequel planned for *That's the Way Love Goes*. What do you think will happen? What would you like to see happen?

ABOUT THE AUTHOR

Daryl C. Diggs grew up in Howell, a small shore town in New Jersey, and now resides in Brooklyn, New York. The idea for *That's the Way Love Goes* materialized during his senior year of college and took two and a half years to fully develop.

A graduate of Morehouse College in Atlanta, Georgia, he holds a degree in finance and currently works as an analyst at a major Wall Street firm in New York City. He enjoys his profession (the one that's paying the bills right now) very much, but has always loved books and great stories. Among the author's favorites are *The Autobiography of Malcolm X* by Malcolm X and Alex Haley, *The Art of War* by Sun Tzu, and *The Iliad* by Homer.

Daryl's hobbies include going to the movies, traveling (please buy some books so Daryl can expand his horizons), playing basketball (he likes to think he can hoop a little), and, obviously, writing. The self-professed "bachelor for life" is also an avid fan of New York City culture and is a frequent museum patron.

GETTING TO KNOW
DARYL C. DIGGS

What was your motivation for writing *That's the Way Love Goes?*

I was in Grand Central Station waiting for a friend during winter break of my senior year of college. I had been thinking about writing something loosely based on my collegiate experience at Morehouse. The friend that I was waiting for was about two hours late, so I had a lot of time to myself. Before I knew it, I had written almost twenty pages. From there, I just kept writing and two and half years later, the book is here.

What was the most challenging part of writing your novel?

I have a very demanding job as an analyst at a bank. Trying to balance writing this book with the business side of self-publishing while still performing well at my job has been a beast. Sleep has pretty much become a memory.

What do you like most about the writing process?

I like the fact that there are no rules. I can do it late at night, early in the morning, or not at all. I love that I can create a fictional world in which I am in complete control. The fate of the characters is entirely up to me.

If you could do anything or be anybody who would you be?

I would want to be a Jedi Knight in a *Star Wars* movie. A lot of people don't recognize *Star Wars* for the exceptional tale that it is. It has so many deep philosophical meanings. The difference between good and evil explained in terms of light and dark. Friendship, destiny, love, hate, redemption—*Star Wars* is deep if you think about it. I also think it would be tight to be in a lightsaber duel. George Lucas, are you listening? Isn't it poetic justice that Samuel L. Jackson, the only black Jedi Master, is a Morehouse man?

Other than you both having brown eyes, is the main character Donavin autobiographical?

I am not Donavin and this isn't *The Best Man!* All of the characters are loosely based on real people that I know and situations I've been involved in, but the characters and situations themselves are fictional. J.R. is the only character who is actually based on a friend of mine. I turned up the volume on him a little, but it's basically the same cat.